GAMEL WOOLSEY (1895–1968), poet and novelist, was born in Aiken, South Carolina, Elizabeth (Elsa) Gammell Woolsey, but in later years took her middle name which she shortened to "Gamel" (a Norse word meaning "old"). Her father was a plantation farmer whose family had influence in the law, the church and education. After her father's death in 1910 they moved to Charleston, where she went to a day school. Despite weak health following an attack of tuberculosis in 1915, she left home for New York in about 1921, hoping to be an actress or a writer. Her first known published poem appeared in the *New York Evening Post* in 1922. The following year she met and married Rex Hunter, a writer and journalist from New Zealand, but they separated after four years. In 1927, while living in Patchin Place, Greenwich Village, she met the writer John Cowper Powys and, through him, his brother Llewelyn and Llewelyn's wife Alyse Gregory. She and Alyse became friends for life, while with Llewelyn she had a passionate and painful love affair.

She left New York for England in 1929, settling in Dorset to be near Llewelyn, where she came to know the whole Powys family and their circle. Parting from Llewelyn in 1930, she married the historian and writer Gerald Brenan in a private ceremony, and they lived together, mainly in Spain, until her death. In 1933 she began an enduring friendship with Bertrand Russell, who wanted to marry her.

Gamel Woolsey, primarily a poet, published very little in her lifetime: *Middle Earth*, a collection of 36 poems, came out in 1931, *Death's Other Kingdom* in 1939 and *Spanish Fairy Stories* in 1944. Her *Collected Poems* have been published since her death. *One Way of Love*, accepted by Gollancz in 1930 but suppressed at the last minute because of its sexual explicitness, tells the story of her painful first marriage; *Patterns on the Sand* (unpublished) recalls her South Carolina childhood. Gamel Woolsey died in Spain of cancer.

Woolsey's novel does contain passing references to lesbianism: its young heroine, who has read of "perverse loves" in Greek and Roman literature, is puzzled to discover that such relationships are enjoyed by women too. Her newly married husband, to whom her "innocence was very dear", cannot bear to see her introduced to his own bohemian world where "the wildest sexual anomalies were a matter of course", but the way of love of which she writes is heterosexual.

Gamel Woolsey was born Elizabeth Gammell Woolsey in 1895 at Breeze Hill Plantation, Aiken, South Carolina. She was the daughter of William Walton Woolsey, an engineer who became a cotton planter after the Civil War, and his wife Elizabeth. She was known in the family as Elsa or Elsie, but later she took her middle name, which was her mother's maiden name, and adapted it to Gamel, a Norse word meaning "old". It is likely that she could claim descent from that eminent butcher's son from Ipswich, Cardinal Wolsey, and indisputable that she was the niece of Sarah Chauncy Woolsey who, under her pen name Susan Coolidge, is widely remembered for her best-selling and still enjoyable *What Katy Did* and its sequels. In view of the censorship of Gamel Woolsey's novel it is ironic, too, that it was another of her distinguished relatives, her half-brother Justice John M. Woolsey who gave the famous judgement in 1933 that James Joyce's *Ulysses* was not obscene and who also, in 1931, lifted the ban on Marie Stopes's *Married Love*, and

ONE WAY
OF LOVE

GAMEL WOOLSEY

INTRODUCTION BY
SHENA MACKAY

PENGUIN BOOKS - VIRAGO PRESS

PENGUIN BOOKS
Viking Penguin Inc., 40 West 23rd Street,
New York, New York 10010, U.S.A.
Penguin Books Ltd, Harmondsworth,
Middlesex, England
Penguin Books Australia Ltd, Ringwood,
Victoria, Australia
Penguin Books Canada Limited, 2801 John Street,
Markham, Ontario, Canada L3R 1B4
Penguin Books (N.Z.) Ltd, 182-190 Wairau Road,
Auckland 10, New Zealand.

First published in Great Britain by Virago Press Limited 1987
Published in Penguin Books 1987

Printed in Finland by
Werner Soderstrom, a member of Finnprint

INTRODUCTION

It is ironic that a book whose original title was *Innocence* should have been barred from publication on the grounds of its sexual explicitness, but that was the fate of Gamel Woolsey's novel, which she was to rename *One Way Of Love*. In 1930 the author wrote to Llewelyn Powys, with whom she had a long and passionate friendship, of her pleasure on receiving her page proofs, but it was to be over fifty years before the work was to appear, as it does here, for the first time. To learn, at that late stage, after correcting the proofs, that a novel will not after all be published is to be placed in a situation rather like that of the jilted party in a broken engagement, with its private pain and its necessity for public explanation; and this was not the only literary disappointment that Gamel Woolsey was to suffer.

Several police prosecutions for alleged obscenity, the most notorious of which was that of Radclyffe Hall's pioneering lesbian novel, *The Well Of Loneliness* (1928), had made publishers jittery in the 1930s, and Gollancz, who had accepted this novel, were understandably wary after the court case involving another of their publications, the novel *Children Be Happy*, based on Christa Winsloe's play, *Gestern Und Heute*, which was made into the tragic and touching film *Maedchen In Uniform*. Gamel in the following year refused to find her *Contraception* obscene. Contraception is a subject which occurs in *One Way Of Love*, and may be one reason why this work—for which, by today's standards, *Innocence* does not seem a misnomer—was deemed unfit for publication.

In later life Gamel Woolsey was to look back on her Southern childhood as on a paradise lost; her poem "Carolina Low Country" paints the landscape of her youth in the regretful blue of Housman's remembered hills, and her land "Where yesterdays are better than today" is his "land of lost content". At times in the cadences of her poetry and prose we can hear the voice of one of Tennessee Williams' sad Southern ladies mourning a ruined past and regretting pretty ephemera, the evanescence of bubbles and balloons; the heroine of this novel remarks, of the paper lanterns which deck a Russian restaurant: "These lanterns are, almost of all things I have seen ... the most perfect symbol of man's pathetic evening gaiety." And in one of her letters to Llewelyn Powys, the author writes plaintively of a bracelet, "It was very pretty like a string of rain drops but I lost it long ago." By the end of the novel, its heroine is learning to depend, like Blanche Dubois, sexually and emotionally at least, on the kindness of strangers.

In photographs of the author taken at about the time that this novel was written there is a vulnerability about the eyes, and about the tremulous mouth, that hints at the sensuality that informs her work; also a transluscence of the skin—perhaps a sign of the tuberculosis that recurred throughout her life—that gives her face the look of a magnolia, that bruises at a touch. Gerald Brenan, to whom she was "married" for many years (she was never divorced from Rex Hunter, the New Zealand journalist on whom the husband in this book is based), dates the melancholy streak in her character from the first outbreak of the disease. It was to necessitate the removal of part of a lung in her youth, and later to make advisable the termination of her pregnancies. These qualities of vulnerability and melancholy, with a certain passivity and a distaste for argument, drew people to her. Alyse Gregory, the American writer and wife of Llewelyn Powys, loved the "little poetess" too, despite Gamel's twice becoming pregnant by Powys and despite witnessing her husband's distress at the loss of the potential children while knowing that she herself could not have a child. Gamel Woolsey is the heroine of Powys' fictional autobiography, *Love and Death*, and although there is evidence that her marriage to Gerald Brenan was happy, her relationship with Powys always cast a shadow. Bertrand Russell was also in love with her for a while.

Gamel Woolsey published only one collection of verse, *Middle Earth* (1931), in what, despite her tuberculosis, was a fairly long lifetime. Having chosen the profession which, perhaps more than any other, exposes its followers to the likelihood of hope deferred making the heart sick, she suffered another blow when, at the age of sixty-one, she sent her sonnets to Faber and Faber, and T. S. Eliot himself sent her a letter of rejection. As he was her favourite poet this was doubly painful, and Gerald Brenan in his *Personal Record* writes of her distress as "the ambitions of a lifetime were shattered and from now on |she abandoned all thought of literary work". He suggests that these wistful verses, full of nostalgia and regret, although poignant and accomplished, were simply not acceptable to the post-Auden world. Apart from *Middle Earth* Gamel Woolsey published a collection of Spanish fairy tales (she and Gerald Brenan lived in Spain for many years), and in 1951 a translation of Pérez Galdó's novel *La de Bringas* under the English title *The Spendthrifts*. Her later book, *Death's Other Kingdom*, is autobiographical like most of her work. Set in the Spain of the civil war, it appeared in 1939 with an introduction by John Cowper Powys, the brother of Llewelyn. The development of her technique from the sometimes naive and uneven, although vivid and poetic, style of *One Way Of Love* is apparent, and the narrative shows the strength and resourcefulness which counterbalanced the gloomy and passive side of her character. She left one more unpublished novel, *Patterns on the Sand*, and some unpublished verse.

One Way Of Love is divided into three parts, and opens with a short prologue in which the heroine Mariana lies in a dreamy adolescent trance-like state in the attic of an old house, listening to the sound of the sea echoing her own restlessness. Like her namesake in *Measure For Measure* and Tennyson's poem, she is waiting, but although her head is full of the heroic legends and fairy tales which will always haunt her, she knows that it is not for a lover that she waits.

The first part of the story finds Mariana, now orphaned, living alone in New York, trying to make a living as a writer. A chance meeting in a publisher's office with Sigrid, a girl of about her own age, changes her life, and she steps, like Alice passing through the looking-glass, into another world. It is characteristic of Mariana that it is Sigrid who leads, and she who follows. In a bravura passage which shimmers with life and energy, the two girls visit the Jewish quarter one bright and windy day. All is glitter and shine; the brilliant tawdry silks and shoes, the flashy jewellery of gaudy glass, the pinchbeck that sparkles brighter than gold. This passage is mirrored much later in the narrative when the girls visit an open-air artists' festival, which the guests attend in fancy dress. Attired in cheap sateen, painted to shimmer for a day, their innocent gaiety is ruined on this occasion when the costumed Bacchus and his entourage turn the evening into a drunken orgy, and they flee.

Her new friend introduces Mariana to Greenwich Village life, and to its writers, musicians and painters, and it is at a party there that Mariana encounters the cold and disdainful Alan Douglas. This scene, in which a famous night-club entertainer, her brown skin powdered a Firbankian purple which lends it a ghastly pallor, goes ululating through the house accompanied by a banjo and guitar, might have been richly comic or satirical in the hands of a different writer, but here it has a sombre surrealism.

"The Snow Queen" was one of Gamel Woolsey's favourite stories, and she borrows, aptly, its frozen imagery for Alan and Mariana's first walk together through a New York transformed to an icy fairy-tale kingdom; early in their relationship Mariana is to wonder if the coldly sensual Alan has, like the little boy in the story, a chip of ice in his heart. They marry one cold morning when the crocuses are in bloom, and although their marriage is punctuated with brief idylls of happiness like crocuses piercing the snow, even when conjoined they remain apart. Mariana observes herself playing a courtesan's role, and is sometimes amused and later alienated when she finds herself "worn with caresses one hour ... scolded like a tiresome servant the next". Alan, or Rex Hunter, for this is a very slightly fictionalised account of the author's own marriage, displays qualities that would now be known as those of a male chauvinist pig, and it is apparent that despite his many affairs he does not really like women. He regards them as inferior, and he recoils from the idea of pregnancy, which he sees as a grotesque distortion of a woman's body. When his lust has been satisfied, sensing his wife's detachment, he feels lonely and betrayed, and she, trapped by the sleeping limbs of the man "she took as a companion for her body in the loneliness of the world", feels alone, "enclosed in his dream and not he in hers". The first part of the book ends with them sailing for England, Mariana in a state of indifference bordering on despair. At night in the cabin her secret mistrust of Alan is roused by the ship's horn that seems to blow a warning, like the horn of one of her legendary heroes, and in troubled dreams she is shipwrecked and swimming endlessly, unable to reach the shore.

In the greyness of a post-war London filled with fog and peopled with the unemployed, Mariana's health deteriorates; she is, like her author, tubercular, and Alan turns a wilfully blind eye to her increasing illness. As the fog which confuses night with day adds to their sense of unreality, they become children again, sallying out of their rooms in the King's Road to all the pantomimes in London, and Mariana's feelings of unease increase when she perceives Alan as "a perverse Peter Pan". If that is true, she herself becomes rather like Snow White when, persuaded by Sigrid who arrives like a good fairy to rescue her, she sails without Alan for America, and lives in a cabin in the woods with birds and animals for her companions.

Reunited in New York, Alan and Mariana take rooms in Patchin Place, where Gamel Woolsey lived and first met Llewelyn Powys. Mariana realises that she is pregnant, and because of her tubercular history, she is advised to have the pregnancy terminated. The tone of this passage is curiously detached, with the heroine taking almost an outsider's view of the proceedings, hovering, as it were, above her own bed. Any grief that the author may have felt at the termination of her own pregnancies is firmly suppressed; there is no hint of moral conflict in one who wrote of herself, "the only religion I have felt was a sort of pantheism", or of any pain apart from the physical. It seems odd that someone who, in her poem "The Flowering Bed", describes in such sensuous detail the conception of a child, could be so unaffected by the experience of abortion, unless it left a chip of ice that numbed her heart, like Kay's in "The Snow Queen". That poem, "The Flowering Bed", and others in the same collection, *Middle Earth*, notably the poignant "For The Body" and "Epithalamium", are every bit as erotic as the novel that was denied publication for its outspokenness.

One Way Of Love is about loneliness. In the final part of the novel Mariana is alone again, about to embark on an affair with a man whom she does not love. Like so many lovers before and after him, he attempts to seduce her with Marvell's lines "To His Coy Mistress", and it is the terrifying couplet, "The grave's a fine and private place/ But none, I think, do there embrace", with its evocation of the loneliness within the wormy grave, which persuades her to let him lead her to bed. The girl who "once had a curious fear that if she were not to find a lover she would be lonely in another world as well as in this: with an eternal loneliness" has discovered that one can be as lonely with a lover as when alone, and, realising that she is about to commit adultery, resolves gaily that she will go to hell and find lovers there—"since I cannot find a true love anywhere".

If there is pathos in Mariana's defiance, like a paper lantern hung against the night, there is also honesty and real courage in her stance; and it is for these qualities, as well as for its value as a small work of art—a bracelet, perhaps, of raindrops—that this lost novel deserves to be found.

Shena Mackay, Surrey, 1986

ONE WAY OF LOVE

A young girl was lying in a house by the sea, on a cot in an attic under the eaves. The attic was dusty and dim and shafts of light from two dormer windows rested on the floor as solid to the eye as Purbeck marble. The house was large and old and the attic was full of worn and broken furniture which had drifted like flotsam out of human life and come to a last resting place unwanted there. There were broken chairs and unsteady tables and darkened pictures in cracked frames, and in one corner near the shabby wooden cot on which the girl was lying a pile of old books with rubbed calf-skin covers still faintly ornamented with antique titles and gilt stars. Many of them had not been touched for fifty years until she had brought them to the light and read them, listening while she read to the sound of the wind and the palmettos rustling like rain in the garden below, finding some secret pleasure in lying hidden in the attic where no one ever came.

To-day she was not reading. There was a great wind blowing from the west: It ruffled the sea below until the waves turned sharply up like fur brushed backward and standing on end. The white clouds driven before the wind passed across the windows and were divided by the small panes into bright parti-coloured squares like stained glass : then suddenly the pattern was gone and the glass became clear and blue.

Mariana could not see the ocean from the bed where she lay. She could hear its monotonous beautiful repetition, but she did not hear it : she had always lived within its sound and could hear it only with a conscious effort now. She had read in books of ' Eternity ' and had somehow identified the ceaseless sounding of the ocean with the far-off roaring of Eternity, beating perpetually upon Time.

Ever since she could remember the sound of the wind blowing about the house as it blew this day had given her a feeling of excitement and romance. She had come to the attic on windy afternoons and lain listening and reading, feeling secret and safe and at the same time in the midst of some adventure. She had always been perfectly happy in her secret life.

But to-day as sometimes of late it was different. She was restless and troubled with vague expectations. She seemed to be waiting for something— but what could she be waiting for ? She was sixteen now : could it be love ? People, she knew, married and lived together and had children. Mariana, brought up on a plantation, knew how animals mated and human beings too. It did not shock or puzzle her. But she did not really know. There was nothing in her mind to tell her what it was. It was merely another of the incomprehensible things in the Universe. In any case it was not what she was waiting for.

Her dark head was full of poems and fairy tales. In fancy she died on many a stricken field, sometimes as Oliver fighting by Roland's side or as Tristram mad with love wandered in lonely forests. But what was this love for which people ran mad? It is reserved in fairy tales for the prince and princess; we are not told that the common people loved. Perhaps, she thought, it is too rare and I shall always be alone, and a vague melancholy clouded her mind.

For some reason a day now three years past came back into her mind. She had waked in the morning feeling ill and found blood on her gown. She knew what had happened to her, but she was unhappy all day and for days afterwards. She felt that her body had betrayed her: life would never be the same any more. She would have this thing returning every month with a feeling of trouble and pain and a vague desire to cry for some unknown reason.

Her breasts had grown fuller and rounder every day since then, until they were now like Nicolette's as firm as hazel nuts. And when she put up her heavy curling hair in the hot summer weather she looked almost like a woman. But her mind was still a child's mind, fanciful and secretive, only sometimes agitated with these new troubling apprehensions that made her awkward and shy.

Impatient of her restlessness and of her inactivity she sat up suddenly on the couch and her eyes fell on the dusty pile of books heaped just at the edge of the shaft of light where she could reach them. She took one up. It was one of the few that were not old, a coverless, backless volume, printed atrociously on rough grey paper. It was a book she knew, a very curious thing called *The Sixth and Seventh Books of Moses*, compiled by some shady Chicago publisher out of old astrological works and Pliny and the Cabala, to sell to the negroes for a dollar. It was full of ancient charms, of pentacles, and magic conjurations.

Mariana fluttered its grey water-stained leaves. " The Angel Athuriel," she read, " will appear as a beautiful and mild young man wearing a chaplet of pearls. He is powerful to give you your desire, and will reveal hidden treasure."

She turned the leaves again, pausing to examine a strange figure of two crossed triangles in a circle surrounded by unknown names. She could hardly make them out, the printing was so bad and the paper so rough. " This charm," the inscription below said, " should be written with butterflies' blood on virgin parchment." Where would Aunt Mahala or Maum' Hester get virgin parchment, she wondered, laughing a little, and what would they think it was ? But though she laughed, she half believed that the charms of this shabby book might be true, might at least have been true once, turning the page again, she read :

"TO BE BEAUTIFUL AND BELOVED.— You must take seven drops of wine from seven cups, seven crumbs of bread from seven loaves, seven grains of wheat from seven mangers. And bury them at the root of a thorn-tree in the dark of the moon, and cut a notch in the bark with a knife made entirely of iron. When the moon is in the first quarter you must come in the early morning before dawn and just at sunrise bend down a bough of the thorn and shake the dew over your head, saying :

" ' Oh ! Thorn Tree, Oh ! Thorn Tree, my trust is in thee.' This charm will make you Beautiful and Beloved."

To be Beautiful and Beloved ! The sea on the shore beat loud and insistent. Mariana heard it even through the veil of accustomedness. If she went up upon the sea, as Homer said, she would go to some country where she would find what she wanted. She did not know where that country would be or what would happen there.

PART I

PART I

Mariana opened a door into a garden. The autumn wind blowing across the closed city court ruffled the gourd leaves climbing in huge patterns on the yellow walls. The square of atmosphere in which she stood was the open grass-covered centre of a city block, and it was full of bright movement. At one end high above her, from window to window, clothes danced upon a line. She heard the sound they made like flags triumphantly flapping, streaming along the air. The wind was like a river pouring over the roofs of the houses in a rushing waterfall. She was surrounded by speed and brightness: everything about her seemed to swirl and sway: the leaves on the ground, suddenly eddying in a whirlpool of wind, danced around her in a ring.

" This is the place where I want to live," she thought. She stepped back out of the airy brilliance of the autumn day into the dark hall.

" Where are the rooms ? " she asked the heavy Italian caretaker. He hardly knew English, but like a horse that has learned the way his slow steps led her up four flights of stairs to the top of the high narrow house and into a room where two large windows looked out again on the wind-filled garden.

The interior of a large city block had been turned into a lawn, but each house had its own little garden, she noticed, as well. The gourd vines with their huge leaves trained to grow up the yellow brick walls gave to the houses that surrounded the four sides of the square, all high, narrow, old and precisely alike, the appearance of a huge stage set, empty and waiting for the play to begin.

The room she stood in was large, newly painted and empty; from it opened a little kitchen and a white-tiled bathroom with a skylight through which the afternoon sunlight poured down upon the white shining floor. It seemed unnatural to find this newness at the top of these winding narrow stairs in this old house, where the rooms were shut away from the outer world and the sound of New York came only as a faint ceaseless roaring from a far-off living sea.

" I will take it," Mariana said. She was sure that she would like living here. The room seemed high and secret. She felt that she could live in it in safety, descending when she wished into the city, and returning again as it were out of the world.

The next afternoon she moved in, bringing a kitchen-table and wicker chairs and a couch, are bought as cheaply as possible from a second-hand furniture dealer. In her trunks and boxes she had a few finer things, curtains of faded rose brocade, pieces of old china, a little table silver, and a mahogany mirror with a carved gilded eagle perching upon it.

She had brought them with her from the South. They were all that was left to her now of her home, of the house by the sea where she had lain one day listening to the wind, wondering to what future country she would go.

She had lived alone with her grandmother then ; and it had not seemed possible that that life would ever cease. But her grandmother had died when she was eighteen, leaving her these few old things she had kept since in trunks and boxes, and the small income, all that was left after Civil War and Reconstruction had ruined the South.

The old plantation house in which they had lived by the sea had been sold, and was now the property of a rich northern manufacturer. Mariana had gone to look at it for the last time the day before his carpenters and painters had begun to renovate it. It stood grey and ghostly at the edge of the beach, surrounded by heavy live oaks hung with Spanish moss. In a lagoon behind it rice was growing wild, the thin spears piercing the shallow water. The scene had the beauty of complete desolation. She had not remembered it like that : when she lived there it had been home to her, and she had not realised how abandoned and wild it was.

She had stood for a long time watching the grey moss waving in the warm sea wind, straining her ears to hear, fixing her mind to keep for ever the look of that house, the sound of that sea she would never look upon, she would never hear again.

The time following her grandmother's death had been sad and difficult for her. She had bitterly regretted the tall handsome old woman who had taken the place of her parents ever since she could remember ; and had felt great grief and a kind of impotent anger to think that her lovely manner was gone for ever with her thin quick fingers and silver hair, while her white widow's caps and the fine old lace she always wore, which seemed no more a work of art than they, still existed unaltered.

She lifted now from the trunk before her a dress of that old lace : she had worn it herself at her first ball when she had come out two years before. It lay across her knees and she forgot to put it away while her mind went back to the days after her grandmother's death, and she remembered how lost she had been in the open world in which she had suddenly found herself.

She thought with amusement (now that she had

escaped from them) of the various cousins who had
kindly offered her a home after her grandmother's
death, and how alarmed she had been at the
prospect of living with any of them ; for her
guardians would not let her have her small income
and live alone until she came of age. Those
cousins—their very names were awful ! Washington Wilkinses and Pickens Johnsons—insisting
perpetually on past grandeurs, absurdly magni-
fying present insignificance. The worst of all was
Cousin George the small town lawyer from 'Up-
State'—too talkative, half-educated and shiftless.

Only one of them was really nice : Cousin James
with whom she had lived for the three years since
her grandmother's death. He had been both kind
and charming. She thought of him now with
tender amusement—a little grey old doctor
reading Horace and Cicero in his dusty office
where few patients came except the negroes who
did not pay but to whom the old man was
indulgently kind.

The difficulty there had been his wife. What a
terrible woman she was ! Animated, pushing,
rushing from one card party to another, narrow-
minded, conventional and mean. She could never
have gone on living in the house with such a
woman : she must have left even if she had not
wanted something different from what Charleston

21

offered her. Somehow she had never been at home there, she had always felt out of place.

They knew it, too, she thought now, remembering the great balls to which she had been taken, and how she hardly knew anyone at them because the old doctor lived completely out of the world and his wife was not, as Charlestonians put it, ''one of us.'' How bored she had been by the nice young men she had danced with ! And how I must have bored them, her mind put in with a flicker of malicious amusement since success at Southern balls had drifted away to the very periphery of the circle of importance now that she was no longer obliged to search for something at them. But what had she been searching for ?

Faintly through the open window notes floated in—a barrel organ in the street was playing an old waltz. The sad sweetness of the air which rayed out through the insistent gaiety of the waltz rhythm troubled her with some unknown desire. She longed for romance, for delight, and vague images of dark dew-wet gardens with white broken statues among green deep leaves filled her mind. Some word should be spoken there : there something should begin. But her imagination failed and the picture faded.

She had come to New York because it seemed the way of escape. In Charleston she had been doomed, she had felt. She would have had to live on, half a dependant, in the shadowy old doctor's house, or get married, and the idea of marrying one of those nice and even charming young men filled her even now at this safe distance with an absurd horror—to marry and settle down in a definite house on a definite street seemed to her still the end of everything. And most of the young men had liked her no better than she liked them. She was not neglected, but she was never popular.

There must be something wrong with me, she thought wistfully, fingering the white dress on her lap, light still with the music to which it had fluttered—I never had but one friend, and he went away.

Hal Edwards had been the only friend and playmate of her childhood. His parents had owned the next plantation. But he was older than she, and had gone away while she was still a child to study archæology and never came back. Now he was exploring Maya ruins in Yucatan, and she sometimes had exciting letters from him with strange stamps and postmarks which stirred her imagination like a sound heard far off.

He had given her his black dog Cæsar when he went away. And for years—until Cæsar died—they would walk along the beach in the evening half hoping to see Hal coming back. But he never came and in the end they almost ceased to look for him, and Cæsar chased fish in the lagoons instead while she played games to herself of heroes and lost battles.

And I never really had any other friend, she thought sadly.

She rose with the thought for some reason and stood before the mirror holding up the white dress to hang at her shoulders like the dress of a paper doll, and looked long and curiously into the glass. A shadowy girl looked back at her : a girl with dark waving hair pulled close over the ears and released in loose curls, and grey eyes, large and wide and strangely slanted like the eyes of a girl in a Kate Greenaway drawing. The mouth completed this impression for it was wide and curled. Now it quivered under her look, flickered and was still again but with a new expression, now it was lifted with a secret smile, a smile of delight in her own youth and hope, a smile as if she was about to greet someone for whom she was waiting.

*   *   *

Mariana's secret hope was to write, even to earn her living in part by writing. She had written poems and a few short stories. She knew nothing of life in New York ; her ideas of literary life were taken from De Quincey's descriptions of London in 1809 or Boswell's chapters on Johnson's circle. She had a very vague idea that she should show her work to some older writer, which one she did not know. She had read most of the English classics in her grandfather's library which had gone after her grandmother's death to his old school, but of modern writers she knew nothing at all. The people she knew in Charleston had only read detective stories or the latest novel.

The old doctor, her kind, vague cousin, had been scholarly, but he seldom read an English book. He read Latin or Greek, and occasionally trifled with Pope or Cowper. He regarded them, quite literally, with Lord Byron whom for some reason he disliked, as light modern authors. Pope he considered as hardly a suitable writer for Mariana—too licentious, but Cowper was perfect. And Mariana to please him read *The Task* and even enjoyed it.

These associations—she thought the next day, as she sat at her window looking out into the autumn sunshine which filled the square between the buildings as wine fills a bowl—would not be of much value in New York. For Cowper after all had died, a hundred years before, she could not go to him and tell him that she liked *The Task* and show him her own work. Perhaps, she wondered doubtfully, that is not the way people behave any more. But the magazines had editors, and the newspapers. She would take some poems and stories to them. She was so shy that it was several days before she could bring herself to go up in an elevator to the proper floor and ask to see the editor of a newspaper which had a literary supplement.

" Will you please write your name here ? " said a weedy office boy. She did it.

" Miss *Clare* to see Mr. *Bennett* about ——" She did not fill in the third blank because she did not know what to say. Presently a tall, thin, austere looking young man came out. He shook hands kindly with Mariana and asked her to sit down. Hesitatingly, apologetically she showed him her poems, and he read them over rather slowly.

" I think these two," he said at last, " are really beautiful. They are original in a surprising, new way. I mean, what you say is. The form isn't original ; it's almost hackneyed. How dare you talk about unicorns ? There ought to be a closed season on unicorns."

He laughed and Mariana laughed. She did not understand him at all. She had read no modern poetry—and unicorns did not occur as often in Cowper or Pope as hares. " I'll keep these two," he said, " and see if I can persuade the editor-in-chief to use one of them. I like them, but I haven't a final say in the matter." He stood up, and Mariana prepared to leave. You are a Southerner," he said. " Where do you come from ? "

" From Charleston," she said.

" Why did you leave it ? " he said, and his tone did not ask an answer.

She smiled and shook hands and turned away. She felt happy, elated that he had liked her poems even in part. The sunlight in the city square could be breathed, could be felt. The yellow leaves on the pavement rustled under her feet. She was alive and young. But suddenly as she walked, feeling the strength of her body, she remembered those doubtful words, " Why did you leave it ? "

*   *   *

Mariana knew no one in New York, but she was not really lonely at first because she was so excited to be there. Only at night when she sat alone in her room and heard the roaring of the city outside her windows she grew frightened ; and she learned not to stay in at night if she could help it.

She was a little afraid of the streets after dark, being unused to going out alone in the South, but she came not to mind and went to the theatre on cheap tickets many evenings by herself. On other evenings when she felt unable to stay in her room she would go to the public library where she could read until ten o'clock.

When she felt happiest she stayed at home all evening and tried to write—but suddenly she would begin to question what she was doing in a city room alone wasting her youth in reading and watching plays, tales of other people's lives. When would she begin her own life ? She would go to bed with a baffled feeling that seemed half physical, as if her blood beat against the walls of her veins.

She decided that she must try to place some more poems or stories. The two that the young editor had praised had been accepted and had appeared, and she had had a cheque for twenty dollars for them. She took the money up-town at once and spent it on a white silk shawl ; in her opinion anything so unexpected as money paid for poetry should be wasted.

One day she chose four poems and a story and made fresh copies of them, typing them very carefully with red titles on heavy smooth paper, and went down-town to the offices of one of the monthlies. She was shown into a large room where typewriters were rattling. A red-haired girl with her hat on and wearing a fur coat was sitting at one of the tables, and a small, dark young man came up to her and said : " Do you mind if I get something here ? " The girl hurriedly moved her things from the table and he took some papers and went out.

Then the girl turned to Mariana with a startled look.

" I thought he was the office boy, and it's the editor ! " she said, beginning to laugh. After a minute's surprise Mariana joined her.

" What shall I do ? " the girl went on, " I want a job, and he'll never give me one now. He'll blame you too for being here."

"Perhaps he doesn't realise what happened."

"Anyone who looked like that would be sure to. Come," she went on, getting suddenly to her feet. "Let's go before he comes back. We'll return in a week or two in different hats and he won't remember us."

With a feeling of gay complicity they went out quickly and ran down the stairs instead of taking the elevator.

It was a bright cold day, people were hurrying about the narrow down-town streets with a mad besotted preoccupation like ants rushing to repair the ravages caused by a walking stick.

"Where shall we go ?" asked the girl. The thought of separating somehow did not occur to either of them. " Shall we walk down to the Battery and see the ships and the gulls ? We can go through the Jewish quarter and Grand Street, I expect you know it ? "

" No, I don't," said Mariana. " I'd love to go."

The other girl seemed quicker, more definite than herself. She was willing to go where she led.

They walked at the quick swinging pace of their long young legs. In a few blocks they were in the Jewish quarter on the down-town East Side. They came to Grand Street.

" This," said the fair girl, " is the Fifth Avenue of the East Side. See the wonderful corsets in the windows and the fur coats. You have to have both here, I don't know why."

But it was the life on the side-walks and the glimpses of the crowded side streets that excited Mariana. The strange, intelligent Jewish faces around her had a look of deep-rooted melancholy from which grew and flowered, as it were, their animation and the pleasure which showed so plainly on their faces in the passing scenes of human existence. She saw an old woman bargaining with a pedlar for a string of onions. Her handsome, shrewd old face was lit with the amusement of the transaction. The pedlar, a poor creature with a crooked back, poured forth a stream of

Yiddish (she supposed) mixed evidently with invective and jokes. The old woman was not slow in replying. They could have played their parts no better on any stage.

Mariana turned from them reluctantly as she passed in their swift walking and saw on the sidewalk by the walls an old man with a white beard, sitting on a stool. As he sat there with people hurrying past and sometimes brushing and knocking against him, with the street cars groaning by and automobiles hooting and carts and horses clattering in the street, he read to himself out of a large book on a little table in front of him, and as he read he rocked himself to and fro with clasped arms and sang to himself a wandering wavering air, which he seemed to make up as he sang it.

" Who is he ? What is he doing ? " Mariana whispered.

But the other girl did not know. She thought he might be a student reading the Talmud.

They left Grand Street and came into a narrow street thick with barrows, around which a crowd of shabby people seethed and shouted. On the barrows was almost everything to wear, to walk upon, to eat, to decorate tenement rooms with, that could possibly be sold to the poorer East-Siders. Mariana through the moving crowd saw

31

at different moments rugs made of parti-coloured goat skins, oranges and grapes, halvah, dusty dates and locust fruit (it amazed her to see the long locust pods for sale here : she had eaten them as a child), battered copper pots and pans, rusty odds and ends of iron, cheap ties and socks, women's underclothes of artificial silk or cotton in bright colours, and the shoddiest shiny stockings, and once, strung all along a wire, glittering glass bowls in which darted surprised goldfish.

She stood still in delight—the scene was so surprising and so rich and strange. The dark, keen faces around her were as foreign as faces in the streets of Nineveh. In the bright winter light it seemed to her as if some Flemish painting of a scene in a ghetto had suddenly come to life and the painted figures were moving before her. Like another Alice into the Looking Glass she stepped into the street drawn by the swirling eddy of its noisy life.

" I must buy something," she said, and the tall girl followed her, laughing.

She parted the people before her, and they closed behind like water round a drop of water. She was a unit in a mass, a cell in a living body whose mind and limbs were busy about the barrows.

The hucksters shouted and waved their wares

before her. Dust rose in eddies, caught by the wind blowing through the narrow streets.

They passed a barrow on which were displayed cheap gilded collar buttons and studs, and mother-of-pearl cuff-links. The next had silk dresses of an amazing cheapness and brilliance ; they were drawn past it more by the current of the tide than by their own volition. The next barrow was a fine one with strings of glass beads flashing in the light, and pinchbeck pins and earrings fastened on cards. The girls stopped there, resisting the tide for a little, and each of them bought a card of earrings for twenty-five cents, flashy, pretty things which they put on at once.

" How absurd it is to buy real jewels," Mariana said, " when you can buy these for a quarter, and they glitter just as brightly—in fact I think the gold is almost *too* bright."

They laughed and, turning, struggled out of the river.

" Let's have tea down here before we start back," the fair girl said. " By the way—what is your name ? Mine is Sigrid Armstrong."

"Mine is Mariana Clare."

" Are you living in New York ? "

" Yes, I've just come from the South. I'm living on Sullivan Street in one of those houses on the big garden."

33

" I live a few blocks above you on Washington Square."

"How odd !"

''No, it isn't really strange, so many young artists live in that part of town.''

*　　*　　*

Mariana and Sigrid rapidly became friends. Their situations were similar. Each had come from a country home to find work and adventure in New York—if they could. But Sigrid had been to college first. She was a little older than Mariana and was more assured and self confident, but they were both very young and very eager and hopeful, not yet dismayed by experience. Anything seemed possible ιo them. Around any corner life might begin, but they did not know how to find it. Mariana often wished there were some actual road to take as in a fairy tale. She wished like the step-daughters of folk-lore she could walk down the first road into another country and meet adventure however alarming. But from the door of her house one street led to Fifth Avenue with its shops and another to the business district. And she knew no way to go that would take her into a more exciting state of existence.

Sigrid thought that perhaps she did. She knew a number of people in New York—girls and young men who had been to the same University, young painters and writers she had met since she came to New York. Mariana met most of them and came to know a few very well. She went to their studios and the painters painted her. She talked with the writers about writing and read their work sometimes published, more often in manuscript. They all believed in themselves, were sure of eventual success.

Some of them were very poor. They lived in the basements—almost cellars they were—under Patchin Place, and kept plants in cracked pots on their window sills to catch the brief sunlight that penetrated there. But they enjoyed it and gave parties in their cellars when the blackened fireplaces were piled with the boxes left outside by the fruit sellers. There was always great competition for these among the artists and the Italian children who wanted them for bonfires in the street. The first to see a box, artist or child, would seize it and drag it along like an ant with a straw. Mariana found a great charm in the hopefulness of their lives, and admired the way in which the poor artists wore their poverty with colour and amusement. But she felt she had not found what she wanted among them. These young men and young women were in no way remarkable. Some slight talent had led them away from their

35

' home-towns ' in the West or the South or ' Down East,' and they put up with their present discomforts because they had the courage and energy and hopefulness of youth. They were ' advanced ' in rather childish ways, liked to talk about sex, a word always pronounced with a capital and separated from the rest of living had strong views of the righteousness of free love and the importance of sexual experiences.

Mariana somehow disliked this. Of course people made love, she had always known it : you had only to go out on spring mornings to see all creation at love—from the birds to the plants, the farmyard cocks, the dogs, the cats, the cattle, the very sparrows in trees. Why should they talk about sex in this awkward heavy way as if it were some technical almost pathological peculiarity of man ? Mariana's vague secret dream about love was to have one lover, to love only one person all her life, in one human relation to give all the small gifts of her withdrawn shy nature. To live with one man always, to have his children, to die and be buried with him. She would have been ashamed to express so common and simple a wish. She was hardly sufficiently conscious of it to express it. She had a curious fear that if she were not to find a lover she would be lonely in another world as well as in this : with an eternal loneliness.

Adventure and romance she wanted but she did not couple them with love. They should be in the nature of life. She still dreamed like any boy of sixteen of stricken fields on which she fought and died, of white horses she rode hunting on early mornings among her father's men. Those things were adventure and romance. Love was another thing.

When one of the young painters asked Mariana to sleep with him she was too surprised even to be shocked. Such a thing as sleeping with someone she was not in love with and did not hope to spend her life with had never occurred to her as possible. She had been vaguely stirred by the young painter. He was a vigorous, original man from some Western farm, large, raw-boned and rather ugly. She felt in him some slumbering potency, a physical emanation seemed to come from him. When they sat together in a room full of people he seemed more alive than the others. He was so real that they seemed to fade into moving simulacra. But his strong desire for her startled her half formed feelings into the light, she was puzzled by them, did not like them because they were new and strange, and drove them out of her mind.

They remained extremely friendly and he sometimes tried to make love to her, but she would not

37

even let him kiss her. He could not be angry because he somehow realised she did not dislike him,
but feared the possibility of his attracting her. He
continued to hope that in the end she might get
used to him, or might suddenly grow up. They all
thought her undeveloped, they could feel that she
did not have a young woman's feeling for men,
hardly a young girl's. She was unripe. Her state
had a charm of its own, but it made no great
sensual appeal to most men.

She realised this in some obscure way, and it
saddened her. She had no desire to be loved by
any of the men she knew or had ever known but
the fact that they felt about her in this odd special
way seemed to mark her out as unsuited to life,
and even perhaps unfit for love.

She met other people as the winter set in. A
handsome dark young woman who lived on the
ground floor below her spoke to her and she found
it was the singer whom she heard practising.
Geraldine Martin was the girl's name, and she
was a Southerner from Virginia. It was Mariana's
accent that had drawn her to speak and she invited Mariana to parties at her studio at which
she met musicians and actors. She liked to sit a
little apart, almost hidden in the corner of a deep
couch, and listen, while the fire lit the room uncertainly, to the music played by some young

pianist or to Geraldine Martin singing the negro spirituals she had listened to as a child.

Geraldine went to Italy to study after a few months ; but she left Mariana a legacy of acquaintances in her world, whom she continued to see.

She liked these young musicians and, a little less, the young actors, but she did not feel that she had found, among them either, the life she wanted. And she was somehow never really with them. They asked her to their parties because she was different, not because they included her among them. She felt an alien, and knowing a number of people now who were attracted by her, even demonstratively friendly towards her, she felt more than ever an outcast.

Her life became gayer. She went to more parties and often went to the theatre and to concerts on tickets given her by the actors and musicians whom she met. But the motion and excitement only drowned for a time her feeling of the emptiness of her life.

One evening in February she sat alone by the window. There was snow in the garden, and the small windows in the houses were all lit and yellow. The gourd vines on the walls were rustling a little in a thin cold wind. A feeling of unrest tormented her. Every limb, every nerve was impatient to be gone. But to go where ? She sat the

39

more quietly for her disquiet, watching the lights of the windows discolouring the snow, and the many little squares across which figures moved vaguely, or curtains waved, and lights went out and came on.

There was a knock at the door and Geraldine Martin entered.

" Come," she said, " there is a party. Kessler is giving one."

" But I don't even know him," Mariana said.

" What does that matter ? This is Greenwich Village not Charleston. Besides he asked me to bring you. We went to the theatre on his tickets one night and he saw you there. It's an enormous party to show his new house and I think you'd enjoy it. He invites everyone he meets. You're quite likely to see the President talking to six Chinese acrobats and a troupe of performing seals."

They dressed and went out and walked down snow-covered streets and crooked alleys until they came to a door in a blank wall into which Geraldine turned followed by Mariana. Then they groped in darkness down a passage between the high walls of houses until they came out into a courtyard. On the other side facing them was a tall narrow house with all its windows blaring forth brilliant lights ; jazz music was playing loudly inside and the sound of it poured out from the windows with the dazzling lights.

Mariana stopped uncertainly, startled by the sudden noise and brightness, and Geraldine laughed and seized her hand and led her in.

A negro maid took their wraps in the hall and they went into the first room : crowds of people were milling about in it, people of all descriptions. Tall attractive girls and young men in evening clothes were standing about, talking among themselves or looking on at the rest. Mariana thought that they were young New York society people, and rather resented their attitude towards the others who seemed so much more interesting.

There were two Chinese students, courteous and evidently amused by the scene : a tall handsome negro in evening clothes with a pretty little brown negro woman, very becomingly dressed in gold cloth and brown fur : some Russians with shaggy hair and thick beards, talking Russian to one another and quite unconscious of the scene around them.

Kessler came hurrying up. Mariana liked him. He had the urbanity of the cultivated Jew, the race that spends riches most richly. He was happy now to be giving so amusing a party and really pleased that they had come to it.

41

Mariana knew that he was the most brilliant of the young theatrical directors, and was glad to find him so attractive and unspoiled.

" Come upstairs," he said eagerly. " *Miriam* is going to sing for us."

Miriam, she knew, was a famous night-club entertainer in Harlem.

He led them up the stairs through the crowds of guests that filled the rooms and wandered on the stairs and in the halls. He knew them all. There were vaudevillians whom he had known in his early days, seedy actors who called him George affectionately, over-dressed theatre managers, rich, reserved Americans, poor artists, well-known writers, famous actors. Geraldine whispered various names to Mariana as they went along. At the top of the house they came to a room which was less crowded.

" She will begin singing here," Kessler told them, " and go up and down through the house. I must go and find her or she will be offended. I know these Stars." He smiled a brilliant, friendly smile that was almost like a boy's grin and disappeared.

Mariana gazed about the room ; she saw a few people who, after the mixture of races she had passed through, looked rather like Old Americans, and standing among them with an alien air a tall

Hindu in a richly coloured turban. On a couch in a corner, by himself, a young man was sitting ; Mariana was struck by the curious brilliancy of his colouring. His hair which curled round his head was bronze and burnished by the lamplight, and his face was singularly clear and bright against the bizarre dull black wall on which he leaned. His cheeks were stained with pure light red, as if some painter had touched his portrait with ver-milion. He had a withdrawn and rather melan-choly look, as if he watched something which no longer had power to amuse him.

As she looked at him the room was suddenly full of people. She was pushed and hurried by this inrush to the corner where he sat, until she found herself sitting beside him with Geraldine on the other side, talking to a young actor whom they both knew.

Miriam had appeared. She was standing in the middle of the room, silent and a little ominous. Her hair which was almost straight, was bobbed and stood out in a thick bush around her small head. She was dressed in a brilliant pink evening dress, and her light brown skin was thickly covered with mauve powder which gave her a brilliant, ghastly pallor. Two young negro men stood beside her, one with a banjo and the other with a guitar. Her body began to sway and writhe

43

and her long mauve arms to wave and struggle with the air. She was half dancing—then her dark painted mouth opened and she began to sing in a raucous, terribly resonant voice a wailing song : " I want to go back to Maryland. I wanna go back to mah M-a-a-a-a-a-a-a-a-m-y."

Mariana listened to her, appalled and fascinated. Her voice was terrible—it had none of the rich beauty so common in negro voices, but the violence of her singing was a crude and powerful drug—a rank essence that drowned everything near it.

Mariana looked at the young man beside her ; his eyes were on the singer, but he remained withdrawn, and he seemed bored and rather disgusted.

Miriam drifted out of the room, still singing, as if she were carried along by the wind of her own motion, her arms and legs waved and jerked in strange rhythms and distorted gestures as if not moved by her own volition but by some overwhelming force possessing her, like the contorted struggles of an epileptic.

She was gone and the people in the room went with her, carried away by her singing.

The young man beside her turned to Mariana : " What an awful wretch ! " he said coldly, condemningly. He had been no more moved by the singer than by a she-cat yowling on a roof.

He simply thought her noisy and offensive. Mariana thought he must lack some sensibility not to have been aware of the strange unpleasant power of the woman ; and at the same time was relieved to find someone so withdrawn from the rowdy life around her.

They began to talk, not noticing the noise and confusion. While the people who had gone away came surging back like the turn of a tide, they talked on quietly as if they were sitting together in the heart of a wood.

*   *   *

Mariana found later that his name was Alan Douglas, and that he was English, but had been taken to Canada as a child. He was a journalist and had drifted about the cities of America for ten years and was tired of the life he led in them. He had a talent for writing for the stage, but lacked the energy to write anything more difficult than a few one-acters which were played here and there by Little-Theatre companies. This much she learned from Geraldine later the same night, but it did not really explain him to her. She did not feel drawn to him. There seemed to be something cold and light in his nature which she did not

45

like, but he interested her more than the young men she knew. Perhaps it was only his brilliant colouring that left a more vivid picture in her mind. He had asked her if he might call when they separated at her door, and a few nights later there was a low knock and when she went to answer it he was there.

She had meant to go that night to the opening of an exhibition which her friend the young western painter was giving, but when Douglas asked her if she was going out she forgot her promise and said she was not.

" Would you come for a walk with me then ? " he said. " It is snowing outside very slightly and there is a little wind. The streets are beautiful. We could walk up Fifth Avenue, it is almost deserted at night."

As they went out the snow met them in a whirling cloud, drawn in by the opening door as if it were seeking light and shelter. The flakes feathered against her face and melted in cold points there. She held up her hand to catch them, trying to see the tiny hexagons before the crystals blurred in melting, but her eyes were too large and vague to catch their minute, sharp definition.

They walked through Washington Square, beautiful in the still snowy night, its fountain

frozen in a perpetual falling. The red brick
houses with their white marble doorways and
window facings were more charming than ever,
old and indistinct behind the thin waving curtain of the snow.

They walked on up Fifth Avenue. The traffic
had almost ceased because of the weather. At
rare intervals a taxi passed them, running slowly
and carefully on the slippery street, the driver
peering like a caged animal through his dim
glass.

They talked easily to one another as they went
of poetry and plays and of their lives, saying
unimportant things which were somehow pleasant.

The snow grew always deeper before them,
flakes swirled down around them and the snow
dust flew up from the drifts into their faces. It
made patterns in the air about them and Mariana
thought of the snow queen and wondered if a
flake of ice had pierced this fair young man's
heart, for there seemed to be something strangely
cold about him in spite of the friendliness of his
crinkling smile.

The houses, all shops and offices, they passed
were empty and darkly shuttered or coldly
lighted to show icy jewels or smooth, glittering
dresses.

47

They felt quite alone, as if they were exploring the great ruins of a deserted New York. The snow had muffled the city sounds and they walked in a whitening silence.

*　　*　　*

When they separated that evening Douglas asked if he might come a few nights later, and she said that he might. As she stood taking off her dress before the mirror and absently looking in it without really seeing herself, she thought of the evening and of the charm of that walk through the silently falling snow. She turned to the window to see the same snow lying white and soft in the garden, a thick blanket for the frozen grass. And looking across the wide garden she saw the yellow lit square which he had pointed out as his window, and while she watched it a dark figure appeared and stood looking out.

A few evenings later he came to see her again and asked her if she would come to his rooms so that he could show her his books. She had often gone alone to the studios of the young painters she knew, so she said without any hesitation that she would come. They walked round two sides of the block and arrived at the house where he lived.

48

He led her up a dark narrow flight of steps and into his room. It was a small room, full of books. There were bookcases along one wall and part of another as far as the narrow couch, but the other two were taken up by the door and the window which let in the murky yellow light of New York until he turned on his green-shaded reading lamp. Mariana sat in the one armchair which stood in front of the desk, while he perched on the edge of the couch, leaning forward over folded arms in a rather strange but graceful position.

He got out a few books to show her, but she realised that it was not for that purpose he had brought her to his room, but to be more at home with her in his own place. And his room touched her because it seemed so poor and shabby and was evidently so valuable to him, since it was a closed place in which he could take refuge and had a window opening out into a garden.

He read several poems to her. She admired the sudden fall of his voice when he began to read poetry. It seemed to mark it out as different, dearer to him than anything else in the world.

" I hope you will come again soon," he said when she told him she must go. He laid his hand on hers. She looked at him with eyes as indifferent and wild as the eyes of an animal. And he knew, as he watched her, that she had never loved, perhaps had never kissed. And something stirred in his rather cold and sensual mind that had never stirred there before—a romantic tenderness. Half ashamed that he had touched her, he quietly took his hand away, and talked so pleasantly and casually on the way back that she almost forgot that he had touched her at all.

*   *   *

He came to see her many times, and often she went to his room. Sometimes they walked together, or together visited the second-hand book shops on Fourth Avenue. She grew used to him as a familiar presence, came to think of him as a friend—a charming rather bookish companion who read her the most beautiful poetry and amused her with tales of the day's adventures in press rooms, or with stories of the odd people he had seen on the East Side. Or he would tell her tales of his childhood, and of his adventures in strange places, for he had travelled over half the world—had been to Australia and worked on a paper in Sydney, wandered about the South Seas and up and down the West of America and had finally come to New York where he worked as a copy reader on a newspaper, writing impassioned scare heads over exaggerated stories with ironic amusement.

Mariana was never quite sure that she liked him. With an intense love for poetry and a dreamy romantic nature, he showed also a coldness and cynicism that repelled her. He was charming, she thought ; but sometimes he angered her and occasionally bored her.

After the first night in his rooms when he had touched her hand, he did not try to touch her or to speak of love to her for two or three months. He could wait. He was engaged in several amorous affairs. He was no lonely boy to be rashly hurried by the urgency of the senses. But his sensual, coldly idealistic nature longed always for something less earthy than his usual girls ; and when he looked at Mariana in her dark cloud of hair with her grey slanting eyes, sometimes he thought that he had found it. And then he was afraid, afraid of troubling and spoiling the thing that he had found—thinking in himself that the utmost caresses he might hope to have of her would bring him less enchantment than the look of her grey eyes, so indifferent and so strange.

And yet he could not help himself in the end. He felt himself swept towards her like any boy in love. He could not let her alone. For happiness or unhappiness he must make love to her if she would let him. Very delicately, very slowly he began.

At first it was no more than the poetry that he chose when he read to her and the tone of his voice when he read it. Then it was only that he held her hand longer when they parted and when they met. Then one night he read her a poem he had written to her. It was a slight but quite charming thing. When he had finished it he laid his hand on hers for the second time. He did not think that anything in her nature started away from him. But when he looked at her eyes they were clear and indifferent, he thought, as the eyes of a wild deer. He lifted her hand to his lips and gently kissed it. It trembled in his as if shaken by a sudden wind. And he felt his own body tremble with lust and tenderness.

So slowly and by such delicate degrees Alan began to make love to her that Mariana scarcely realised what was happening. She became accustomed to have him hold her hand, and then to have him stroke her hair, and kiss her hand, and even kiss her hair. And Alan wooed her as wild animals are wooed to come near, patiently, gently. But it was not calculation that made him so slow, so careful, not knowledge that this was the surest way to have her in the end, but a sensitivity of dawning love that made him feel he must never frighten her, must give her no psychic shock. And he had had so many loves—so many times warm flesh had welcomed him and he had tired of it. It was better, he thought, to sit in the dusk with this fawn of the woods and learn to touch her hair.

But from kissing her hand and kissing her hair he came at length to kissing her mouth—tenderly his mouth dreamed over hers. He felt his passion diffused in the air about them as if they were enclosed in his dreamy life as in some warm air of spring. It almost hurt him by its sweetness. Mariana felt a breath of romance—some old story was being told her, some song she could not remember filled her thoughts with a vague happiness like a dim memory of past sorrow and pain.

Alan persuaded her in these early spring nights to lie on his broad couch with him while they talked in the yellow dusk or he read aloud. He kissed her and kissed her over and over. He taught her to lie with her head on his breast, gently held inside his arm so that she could feel the rise and fall of his breath and hear his heart knocking at her ear. But he did not try to make love to her more passionately then. He could not bear to. This was so sweet.

And still he knew it must happen in spite of him. The spring was advancing, there would come a night when he could no longer hold in his lust to serve his dreamy passion.

53

And now Mariana knew it too. She did not want it to happen. She wanted to stay in this early morning world. But she thought it would happen in spite of her and in spite of them both. She had denied life, had refused love when it was offered her. She could not refuse it always. She would not struggle against it any longer—this tide of life which she could not understand. She would let it carry her where it would. Perhaps her longings, her loneliness would be assuaged if she would but go with it.

But when Alan tried to make love to her more passionately, more definitely, she would not let him and he gave it up for the time. But he caressed the tips of her young breasts and felt the points of them rise up like darts against him. Lust keen and painful stabbed the sweetness of his dream.

One black, windy night Mariana sat looking out into the court. The crying of the wind made her strangely restless. Oh ! was this all of life ? She was alone, alone. There was nothing. She had refused love, had always denied it. But was there anything more ? Would she ever feel passion ? Perhaps if she would let Alan really make love to her, take and possess her body, she would learn to love him. For she was drawn to him, he charmed her. To-night she longed to feel his mouth lying

upon hers. If he came to her now she would go
with him, she would not be afraid to-night. She
would be his equal and match limb for limb.

On the other side of the court she saw his
yellow window and across the dull square of light
a crooked leafless bough. Slowly she went to bed.
My bed is narrow, she thought, like the bed of
some girl in a ballad.

> *It is cold winter night—*
> *Thou and I must lie alone—*

She lay not sleeping, restless and unhappy.
Loneliness seemed to her that night like a black
hovering bird which she must drive away. All
night she wished that he would come to her;
but he did not come.

The next evening Alan knocked at her door.
" Will you come over to my rooms ? " he said.
" I have one or two things to show you." He
spoke with a too complete carelessness, which
showed his anxiety ; but she did not notice it.
She had forgotten her restlessness—it had passed
away as if it had never been—or so it seemed.

They walked through the court. The winter
was almost over now, but the air was very
cold.

Once more Mariana lay on Alan's bed while he
read aloud to her. But finally he put out the light

and they lay in the yellow dusk. Slowly Alan drew her to him. Softly he caressed her hair, her neck, her breasts, her shoulders. She quivered, but she did not resist him when he laid a trembling hand between her thighs. Long afterwards when she read *Ulysses* she was to recognise for the first time what something in her sad, young mind kept saying as she stiffened her body and bit her lips not to struggle or cry out against the strangeness and the pain. For the small, wise voice of her mind kept saying sadly—" It might as well be he. It might as well be he."

Later that night when Alan left her at her door he was troubled and tender. It seemed to him that her wide eyes looked at him with reproach.

But she talked quite happily and carelessly. Tired and sleepy, half in a dream she leaned against the wall just inside the storm door, while he kissed her again and again. She wondered why she had so struggled against something so simple—why he was so troubled and solicitous— for he had only hurt her a little. And what else was there to trouble about ?

And the next day it still seemed very un-important. She was no longer a virgin, but nothing that mattered at all had happened. Her nature, her personality was the same. Her face was the same.

Sigrid coming in to see her saw no difference and greeted her just as usual. And Mariana marvelled that something so serious, she supposed, so fatal, could leave no sign upon her face, and no shadow on her mind. She had not turned overnight into a woman. She was the same girl. She had slept deeply and waked quietly. After all nothing had happened really—not anything that mattered.

Sigrid had come to invite her to go to the theatre on press tickets. " I have four tickets," she said. " I must take mother, you know she's in town, and shall I ask Alan Douglas, would you like to have him ? "

" Yes," Mariana said. She had no particular feeling about it. She felt indifferent whether he came or not. She was more interested in seeing the play, a German expressionist play she had heard much praised.

She asked Sigrid to bring her mother to dinner with her before the play. Sigrid's mother was a fair, handsome Swedish woman who had been brought up on an isolated farm in Varmland, and was full of strange tales of the peasants she had known as a child : Mariana loved to hear them. Now she began to tell a story over their coffee.

" The girl had a baby the next winter, and her father *shoved* her away from his door."

57

Mariana and Sigrid listened intently, but the story had no hold in their lives. It made a dark picture on the air for a moment and then slipped away.

Alan was knocking at the door already, and they hurried up-town to the theatre.

The play that night was a revival of *Johannes Kreisler*. The curious arrangement of the stage fascinated Mariana. Scenes appeared here and there, on the floor of the stage, in the air. Suddenly they glowed out of darkness. The story was happening in that place. The light defined it for a few moments, then gradually withdrew, and all at once another scene appeared in the air above it, caught in the narrow light for a little while.

To Mariana they seemed to be happening in her own mind as if her attention caught fragments of stories, scenes from books, fancies of her own, and lit them brightly until her attention flagged or wandered and another scene appeared.

She sat quietly beside Alan, sometimes accidentally touching him, but not moved by his nearness. Yet she had a pleasant consciousness of another fanciful mind that included this scene and with hers was included by it.

They watched Johannes Kreisler—that is Hoffman—teaching his first love to sing, watching his last love singing on the stage. And she felt a current of romance that ran deeply, hiddenly under her mind, but did not flow towards Alan. And she thought abstractedly, almost with indifference, it was a mistake : and sadly, This is not the way I wanted it.

On the way back from the theatre they left Sigrid and her mother in Washington Square, and went on in silence. Mariana could think of nothing to say now that they were alone together. She felt only that too much had happened between them the night before, more than she had wanted to happen, more than their feeling for one another justified. She felt oppressed by the weight of it.

When they reached her door Alan went on for a few steps though she stopped, then he paused too and said hesitatingly :

" Come to my place a little while, Mariana, I do want to talk to you for a few minutes."

She was tired, she did not want to go, but to please him she followed him down the street and up his narrow stairs. He did not light the lamp, but his room was dimly lit with the light of the city. He took her coat and her hat and put them hurriedly aside. She sat down on the couch and he stood in front of her. " You're all right, Mariana ? " he said. " You feel all right ? "

" Oh, yes," she said calmly. " I'm quite well."
He sat down on the bed beside her and took her
in his arms. He pulled her head down upon his
breast and held her quietly for a long time. It was
Mariana who moved at last. She was uncomfortable, but the slight movement of her body pushing
against him roused him unbearably. He pulled
her gently on the bed and lay beside her. Caressing
her breasts and kissing her mouth he felt his
desire mounting. Slipping his hand under her
skirt he stroked her thighs and tried to pull them
apart, but she struggled away from him and sat
up straight.

" What is the matter, darling ? " he said.
" Don't you like me to make love to you ? "

" No," she said gravely, " it hurts."

And this childish attitude of his mistress enchanted him. Moral objections, psychic repul-
sions might have annoyed him, but this childish
apprehension seemed to him infinitely pathetic
and touching. Resolutely controlling himself he
tried to reassure and persuade her. He laid her
down again gently on the bed beside him and,
tenderly holding her hand against his breast,
whispered in the dark.

" But my little girl, it only hurts at first. Didn't
you know ? I have to hurt you at first, I can't help
it. I didn't know I hurt you so much, my poor

darling. You should have told me. I'll be so gentle
to-night. It will be better if you'll let me have you
to-night. I'll be so gentle. And I'll teach you to
like it, my darling—my little love ! Soon you'll
like to have it."

He whispered tenderly, urgently. He could
hardly control himself. And quieted by his mur-
muring she let him pull back her dress and caress
her legs—let him gently pull her legs apart and
caress her between the thighs. At first he hoped
to rouse some sensual pleasure in her body, but
he realised in a few minutes that she was too nervous and resistant. He gave it up for the moment
and began again to hold her quietly and reassure
her. He thought with an odd thought, half amusement but all tenderness, that it was like trying to
persuade an unwilling child to let you take a
splinter from its leg. And now he was almost
telling her that it was for her own good. And he
was ashamed because he knew she did not want
it, did not want it at all. It was he who wanted to
do it. To her it seemed quite unnecessary and ex-
traneous. He laid his hand on the soft flesh between her thighs, and then he could resist no
longer. He pulled himself over her and his body
found its way into hers. He drove his body deep
into her again and again. He felt her shrinking
and quivering under him. And the knowledge

that he was hurting her gave him the most exquisite, the most tender pleasure.

*   *   *

It was a long time before he taught Mariana to like his love-making. She did not resist him any more—and soon it did not hurt her at all, but she could not see any reason for it. She had been happier when they lay in the dusk together quietly. She wished they could go back, but his passion for her seemed to increase every day. When they were alone together she was always in his arms.

She liked to lie so closely held that her heart knocked at his and his at hers. Locked in a dreaming embrace they would lie speechless while dusk deepened to night. But Mariana knew even while she lay so closely held, letting his arms shut out the world, that she was enclosed in his dream and not he in hers. Her dream was the old dream that she had dreamed within the sound of the sea long ago, and it was unpeopled. No face had ever come into it. Close as she lay in his arms, in her dream she was wandering alone.

Alan had never had a girl so inexperienced and

62

so young. He found that he must do everything for her. He went to see a friend who had studied medicine, and with his help became quite learned in methods of contraception. He tried to protect Mariana's young body against the power of his manhood, but she was shy and unwilling, and his inexperienced hands hurt her.

For several nights he had hurt her. Then one evening when he tried to protect her again, she begged him not to touch her and began to cry with nervous irritation. He was very distressed. He wondered why nature and man had put so many difficulties in the way of physical love, for he must protect Mariana against having a child. The thought of a child growing in her body, changing its shape, making her ugly and ill was horrible to him. And the responsibility of a child— a child in New York. But to protect her, he must force on her these tiresome measures that frightened and distressed her. And yet when he held her, comforting her, close in his arms—all his lust turned for the moment into tenderness—he felt such love for her as he had never imagined, because she was so young, so like a child. He realised some odd quality in her, some strange and fundamental innocence that nothing he could do would ever change. And these contraceptives for which he had always felt a disgust, half moral and half æsthetic, seemed to him now, in the tenderness of his lust, no more horrid and no more unnatural than a bandage.

For a long time Mariana could not learn to like the intimacy of love-making ; it had become associated in her mind with pain and difficulty, and as yet her body had no pleasure in it ; but she responded to Alan's kisses. She liked to be kissed and to be caressed. As the weeks went by she began to be conscious of a new feeling. When he possessed her his body troubled her : she was stirred and agitated : afterwards she was filled with melancholy and anxiety. She wanted to cry, to grieve for some trouble, some disappointment, she did not know what. Alan's very hands upon her hair irritated her. For weeks she felt this distress whenever he touched her.

Alan noticed her melancholy and understood it better than she did. He tried more and more to please her body. Tried to stir her with intimate caresses—long-drawn kisses—sweet words whispered while they lay locked together.

One day when the leaves had begun to bud and the weather was wild and dark, Mariana sat all afternoon looking out on the windy weather, trying in vain to write. Night closed with a gusty wind knocking at the windows. She was as restless as a bird waiting for a mate in the empty forests.

Alan came to take her to his rooms. As they lay together on his couch in the tender preliminaries of love-making, she felt tides of excitement mounting in her blood. For the first time she wanted him to take her, to possess her.

And when at last Alan came in to her, then as his body moved in hers, she was conscious of a new feeling, so extraordinary that she clung to him in fear. She seemed to be striving towards some goal, struggling with every limb, with all her blood to obtain something infinitely desired. The core of her body was shaken, convulsed. Something seemed expanding within her, growing like a fruit, trembling in the wind, till suddenly it burst like the head of a soaring rocket into a thousand little bright shoots of delicate pain that ran from her womb along every nerve so that she cried out, clinging to him in fear and wonder, shaken unbearably by this pleasure too like agony. Then she found herself sobbing in his arms, sobbing with excitement and fright and strange relief.

Alan wanted to marry Mariana, but he was afraid. He had had many girls—and he had always tired of them, or they had grown disappointed in him and had gone away. He was an idealist of a coldly sensual sort. He dreamed of some impossible perfection in amorous relations. With each new girl in the glamorous enchantment of lust, he thought he was in that world of romance made by his mind from physical longing and poems remembered. Then as his lust cooled and he found himself with another human girl, saw her body's flaws and her spirit's imperfections, he turned away hurriedly, shocked by this evidence of the world's ugliness. Disappointed and disgusted, he retired to his books and to his vague dream until the stirring of his blood led him again along the same path. He took small interest in girls unless he could somehow fit them into his life's illusion, unless he could, even if only for a few hours, lay on their shoulders this garment of romance. But this garment could be cut in many shapes, and so he had had many girls. And women often loved him because this vesture that he gave them was beautiful, and they could not know that it would not wear.

But still, in spite of everything, he believed that he would always love Mariana. He could not think that he would ever tire of her soft delicate body. The odd things she said, her strange fancies, her childish fears enchanted him. He wanted to keep her for ever. Even if he wronged her in doing it he must marry her. He must put a legal and permanent seal on these passing physical unions. The world around them seemed in flux, changing and fading. He must save this sweet thing he had

66

found. He must somehow keep it unaltered.

Mariana did not really want to marry Alan in spite of the excitement of her waking senses—these new thrilling sensations that ran through her body sometimes now when he possessed her, this strange pleasure, keener than all other delights of the world. She did not want to marry this man, to be with him always. But it was so sweet to be loved, to have a companion for her body in the loneliness of the world. Even if his thoughts were not like hers, even if the essential creatures of their spirits should never meet, she would no longer go uncompanioned. She had given up this search for the impossible, she would take what the world had given her, what compensation it had to offer for abandoned hopes. And her physical unions with Alan had given her a feeling of loyalty and of obligation to him. She had committed herself, she felt, to serve his happiness. She must go on with the thing she had begun, since it was too late to turn back.

On a chilly spring day when the crocuses were in bloom in the parks, Alan and Mariana went down to the city hall and were married. An official with a Bowery accent recited the marriage service to them in a great empty stone-walled room with stone flowers carved on the cornices. " If any person here present know any reason why these

67

persons should not be joined "—*should not be joined* said the echoing room. Mariana shivered. But she was touched by the words of the marriage service so unexpected here. " For richer for poorer, in sickness or health till death do you part." What was this she was promising ?

They went out past the young blossoms in City Hall Park, in bloom in spite of the cold winds. " We'll walk home," Alan said, " and buy our dinner on the way."

Broadway stretched before them out of sight. It seemed as long as the future to Mariana's wondering eyes ; where was she going with this strange young man ?

* * *

She had promised to go to an 'evening' at the apartment of her friend Ligeia, a young Russian writer married to a Russian editor. She felt that she must go even though it was her wedding night, for Ligeia had sent her a special note asking her to come " because I am born to-day."

She wanted to take Alan, but he would not come with her. He was lost in a dream—meeting people would only wake him and spoil his wrapt happiness. He walked with her as far as Ligeia's door and they bought a pot of red tulips for a birthday offering.

The small rooms were full of Russians. Mariana was the only American there. She sat next to Ligeia by the tea-table, and talked to her in English, or to the few Russians who spoke English or French.

A tall, white-bearded old man came over to sit beside them. He had been a captain in the Czar's army, but had been exiled for his radical opinions and only recalled at the end of the War, in time to become a general under Kerensky. Ligeia had told Mariana that Russians called him ' the old ikon ' because he was so honest that people felt one might swear by him instead of a holy image.

His bearded face was frank and good, as if the white beard were only a mask he had put on to hide unalterable youth.

He began to tease Ligeia in Russian. Mariana leaned back against the wall and watched the scene. David Zaharitch, Ligeia's husband, had begun to sing a folk-song in a rich, sweet voice, and the other Russians were joining in a chorus, uncertainly, but with vigour. Can this possibly be New York, Mariana thought, or am I translated ? The faces around her were so foreign but so kind, more human because more aware of humanity than other faces. I think this is what men are like, she thought, when you find them. We are not so man-like as this, the coldness and

69

stiffness of our minds deforms us. Among us eyes are looking for a forehead, and arms for a body. But these people are all in one creation.

" I must go," she whispered unwillingly to Ligeia. She did not want to go. She was happy and at home here, though she could understand hardly a word of the speech around her.

" You must not go yet," said Ligeia indignantly. " No one goes. It's early."

But Mariana went. Ligeia came to the door with her. There was always so much to talk about and they lingered there. "There's a Russian exhibition this week at the Brooklyn Museum," Ligeia said. " Will you go with us on Saturday ? "

" Yes," said Mariana eagerly. Then she remembered with a shock that she was married. Alan would not want to go to an exhibition of Russian painting, perhaps she would not be able to go. She would have to explain, but not to-night. Ligeia stood holding her hand, her beautiful dark eyes rather maliciously questioning.

" When I told your fortune last time," she said, " there was a fair stranger, and an enchanted guest. Do they come yet ? " She laughed a gay childlike laugh.

" No," said Mariana beginning to laugh too, with a feeling of delight at being still after all a young girl with another girl. " I think you will have to be the enchanted guest yourself to make your predictions come true."

She kissed Ligeia. " It's nice you came," said the Russian, her pretty broken accent had suddenly a wistful sound. The underlying Slavic melancholy of her nature had taken possession of her, and she stood quiescently watching Mariana who almost ran down the dark stairs in her fear of being late and keeping Alan waiting.

When she went upstairs Alan was waiting for her. He had stayed in her rooms quietly reading all evening. She had never slept with him before, never gone to bed with him and she felt shy. Alan was in bed first and put out the light. Mariana had undressed in the bathroom. At the edge of the bed she dropped her dressing-gown and, groping in the dark, felt for the edge of the covers, but Alan was expecting her and she was received in his arms. She was tired—she wanted to lie still and sleep. But she was enfolded by Alan's desirous body. And she tried to kiss him back as he kissed her, to meet his limbs with hers and share his passion—for was this not her wedding night ?

But it was charming to wake the next morning just at dawn, and see her own dark, curling hair mixed with Alan's short, bronze curls. She laughed secretly at his face because it was crinkled in sleepy protest against the brightness of the day. Her head lay still on Alan's shoulder. They had slept all night in one another's arms. The early sun and the chilly spring air came in through the open windows.

Alan stirred, murmured inarticulately and pulled her closer to him. He lay without speaking while tides of love and desire for her seemed to pour through his blood. Then he raised himself on one elbow and looked down at Mariana. She smiled back at him and saw that his eyes were heavy with desire.

The hour when dreams are deeper and winds are colder.
The hour when young love wakes on a white shoulder.

—he whispered to her. Half asleep she felt no desire. The morning air, clear and fresh like spring water, chilled her face and her bare arms and neck. But her body lay warm and softly sunk in Alan's arms : relaxed and still drowsy, she yielded to his body. His passion was perfectly meaningless to her in this hour, but she did not dislike it. It neither hurt her nor troubled her, and when it was over she stretched out her arms in the chilly morning air with the careless, indifferent happiness of a young animal waking at dawn.

* * *

Mariana wrote to announce her marriage to a few friends and relatives in the South because she thought her grandmother would have done so ; but there were none who would care very much, except Cousin James, the kind, little, grey doctor. He sent her a silver bowl which had belonged to her great grandfather ; and another cousin, an old lady in Georgetown whom she had never seen, sent her a pair of earrings of twisted gold set with goldstone and ivory in a pattern of stars.

Alan had always made profession of his dislike of the institution of marriage and the custom of domesticity. But his pride in Mariana made him desire to show her as his wife to his old friends ; and like a naturalist who has added to his collections the rarest of butterflies, he was anxious to be praised and to be admired for having won to his bed this strange and beautiful creature.

One day he brought James Davenant, the odd and erudite young Englishman who was his only masculine intimate in New York, and received with complaisance his congratulations on her beauty and breeding. Alan was obliged to go out while his friend was there, and Davenant in his nervousness at being left alone with Mariana picked up a volume of Shakespeare.

" Will you read to me ? " she said. She had been warned that he was happier with books than with people. But it seemed to her a pretty and courtly sort of erudition that made him choose *Romeo and Juliet*.

On another day Alan brought a girl he knew to tea. Mariana supposed that he must have a particularly intimate and tender affection for this girl. He always spoke of her with great gentleness, but without any inflections that could suggest love or passionate interest. And he brought her to see Mariana rather as one might bring a little cousin from the country.

The girl carried a gift of a jar of growing pansies. She was a pretty and gentle creature, and there was something in her manner very tremulous and shy. She approached Mariana as if she admired her and was afraid of her, almost as if she was in the presence of a princess and alarmed to be there. Something in this tremulous intensity of manner made Mariana feel sure that the young creature was in love with Alan. And she was filled with pity. The thought that her marriage to Alan might so seriously have shocked and injured this sensitive young creature made her very sad. To take something that another wanted, something so irreplaceable !

And was it a thing that she really wanted herself ? She did not know. It might have meant so much more to her, Mariana thought

74

with regret. The girl looked at her without envy and without jealousy, only with this trembling, wondering gaze like that of some small and helpless animal.

Another day Alan brought a very different person to see her. She had often heard him speak of this girl, too. Her name was Mary Moore. She was very tall and graceful with dark hair and eyes, and was a fairly successful young actress. Alan had known her very well for six or seven years. Mariana did not know what their relations had been, but took it for granted with no great curiosity about it that they had at one time been lovers, but had long ceased to be so since Mary Moore had been married for two years to James Shearn, a rather weak, rather pleasant young actor.

But the manner of Mary Moore towards her made Mariana think that for her at least the old affair was not entirely over. She sensed curious antagonisms in the girl, to herself as the new beloved, to Alan as one who had done a wrong, forgiven possibly, but not forgotten. And yet she was sincerely cordial, almost affectionate to Mariana. She seemed touched and fascinated by these young lovers. When she looked at them as they sat together on the sofa, but carefully at extreme ends of it, her smile was singularly sweet.

It twisted her slightly drooping, embittered mouth into a lovely curve. But once Alan's look when it fell on Mariana grew heavy with desire. Mary Moore caught his expression and her face changed as Mariana watched it. Her mouth took an angry, bitter twist. There was a look in her eyes at once anxious and furtive, like the look of a rat. Mariana turned away. She was embarrassed, and she felt anger and even a sort of disgust for Alan because he had exposed her to this. That someone could be jealous of her seemed to her degrading. She was glad when Mary Moore left soon after, making them promise to come to dinner so that Mariana might meet her husband.

Mariana felt a sort of physical dislike for Alan when he came back from escorting their visitor to the door ; but Alan was too intent upon love-making to notice it. Their occasional visitors always whetted his desire by the enforced distance kept during their presence.

With Mariana on the couch beside him, alone with her at last after these two hours spent in tea and conversation, he had no time for words, no leisure from the urgency of his lust to notice her preoccupation ; and she, who had almost a courtesan's desire to please, even at the sacrifice of her own pleasure, showed no sign that his kisses and his caressing hands and his final intimate

76

embraces did not please her. He saw that in spite of his lingering caresses she did not share his ecstasy, but he thought that she was too tired. It was not many hours since he had embraced her, and he had had her that morning in bed as well as the night before. He was full of regret to think that he might be really hurting her, exhausting her by this lust of his that seemed to him, when he was with her, as uncontrollable as the lust of a stag in rut.

But in these hours when his desires were satisfied for a time and his body had ceased its impatient demands, the tenderness born of this same lust made him anxious for her. She seemed very tired to-night. Was she asleep? Carefully he turned his face a little towards her, trying not to disturb the small head cradled in the cup of his shoulder. He saw her eyes, large and dark, staring at the ceiling. And something in the wide and melancholy gaze which he caught before she saw his look and smiled for him, told him that in spite of his arm around her, she had forgotten that he was there. He felt alone and betrayed.

The apartment bell rang loudly, brutally. Mariana sprang up hurriedly, and pushed the button. They were going out to dinner with Jack Hasty, a New York friend of hers, whom she had seen a good deal of lately and very much liked.

77

Could he be here already, and she was not dressed ! Mechanically Alan began to straighten the cover of the couch, rumpled and disarranged by the movement of their embracing limbs, while Mariana hurriedly smoothed her tangled hair before the mirror with a golden eagle perched upon it.

Hasty had climbed the stairs before they had quite finished trying to conceal the traces of their love-making.

Mariana and Hasty greeted each other warmly, and Alan felt at once that their friendliness was excessive. Mariana showed too much feeling in greeting mere acquaintances. After all she is an American, his mind said slightingly, an English girl would be more reserved. He liked Hasty, a pleasant young painter, but he made his welcome unusually stiff to atone for the warmth of Mariana's. Hasty took them to a restaurant where they could dance. He was fond of dancing though he was a little lame from an old injury. He hated being lame, and felt that his power to dance in spite of it was a triumph over his lameness. He particularly liked dancing with Mariana who was light and pliant and yielded almost unconsciously to the will of her partner's body.

Alan did not care much about it. As they walked to the restaurant they began to talk of dancing, and Alan said that it was a sign of women's inferiority that they could so easily be taught to dance in choruses, all kicking at the same instant, standing on their heads at the same instant, falling over backwards at the same instant. Even more than prostitutes it showed how malleable women were : they could be taught to do anything—like trained seals. They would follow any movement, imitate anything, like monkeys.

Mariana felt entire antagonism to Alan as he talked. How tiresome he is, she thought unsympathetically, knowing all the time that there was some trouble in his mind, but not caring about it.

At the restaurant, while they waited for the first course, she danced with Hasty.

Hasty, in spite of his lameness, danced well. He made the variations of the dance serve his halting step so that his dancing seemed to his partners and to the spectators original and graceful. But he was always conscious of a difficulty, of the adjustment he was making ; and it came to be a symbol of life to him, this dancing in spite of lameness, this handicap which he was never allowed to forget. It seemed to him sometimes that the lameness was in his mind as well, a difficulty against which he thought.

79

But now, dancing with Mariana, he had almost forgotten the lameness of his leg, and her sympathy had exorcised the halting of his thoughts. They were enjoying themselves, talking and laughing as they danced ; and they had forgotten Alan.

He watched them from their table as the jazz orchestra redoubled its efforts before coming to an abrupt pause, and he felt the sick irritation of jealousy. He was not jealous of Hasty as a man. He knew that Hasty and Mariana were not in the least in love with one another ; it was not that. But again in the spirit Mariana had deserted him.

A few nights later they went to dinner with Mary Moore and James Shearn. Mariana knew that they were neither of them very good or very successful on the stage and she was surprised at the size of their apartment. It was decorated handsomely but without much taste. Shearn mixed cocktails, and they each had one. Mariana felt a little dizzy after hers, but noticed that Shearn and Mary Moore drank several. They both were gay and talking rather loudly. Alan refused a third cocktail, but he seemed to be enjoying himself. He knew many of the theatrical people of whom they were talking, and if he did not know them, he knew about them. Their talk was almost all personalities, theatre gossip. Sometimes they spoke of plays, but generally only if they knew the actors. Mariana was a little bored by the gossip. It gave her a feeling of futility. An entire evening spent in talking of the personal oddities of unimportant people seemed rather a waste of time. She was surprised that Alan, usually so æsthetically particular in his interests, seemed to enjoy it all greatly. She realised then that the Alan she had seen was only part of a more complex personality. How could it be otherwise ? His greatest pleasures might be literature and love, but after all he earned a living as a successful newspaper man. Part of his mind must be frivolous and cynical, or he could hardly be successful at such a trade ; could never have endured following it for so many years.

But Mariana was impressed by Mary Moore. In the candle-light she looked very beautiful. She laughed often, and her laughter lifted the disappointed droop of her mouth. Even in these personalities that they were discussing her humour was delightful, her descriptions of people genuinely amusing and not malicious. She seemed to like human beings and to have the lowest opinion of them. As the evening wore on her remarks about human relations were sometimes so startling that Alan looked anxiously at Mariana and kept changing the subject which kept as obstinately changing back again.

" She lived with two young men," Mary Moore was remarking, " they liked each other very much, in fact people said they were in love too. But they didn't like it when she took another lover as well. He was a prize-fighter. It all split up after a year or two. I don't know what became of the boys, but she became completely Lesbian. She has a perfect court of young girls now. You have to push your way through them when you want to go back stage."

Mariana listened rather puzzled. She had read of perverse loves in Greek and Roman literature, but she had somehow failed to understand that women were like that, and the word *Lesbian* so used she did not understand. She was not shocked, only a little puzzled and not particularly interested. But Alan finding himself unable to restrain the conversation soon took her away.

He was rather silent as they walked home. It seemed to him that through the nature of his past life he was exposing Mariana to situations in which he did not want her to be placed. Her innocence was very dear to him. He could not bear to see her initiated through him into a world where the wildest sexual anomalies were a matter of course. He believed in much indulgence to unusual aberrations of sex. He did not disapprove of

82

them. But he did not like to think that Mariana had even heard of such things.

That was the devil of marriage. If he and Mariana were not married he could have continued to go to see Mary Moore without her. Mariana would have been safe. He did not want to give up his old friends completely. And until he had seen Mariana with them he had not realised how cheap and unpleasant some of their talk was. Had it always been so? Was it only his recent association with this more sensitive young creature that had made him realise it? But Mary was really a remarkable woman. She was coarse in her talk and had got much coarser these last two years and she was rather careless in her behaviour, but she had integrity of character, was generous to a fault and with unusual charm had an alert eager mind. He had wanted Mariana to know her. Of course he was not in love with her any longer—after two years apart he felt no more than kindliness ; but even in decency he could not stop going to see a girl who had been giving the wildest proofs of her love for him only three years before. And how she had loved him ! She would have scrubbed floors for him. In fact she had, he remembered—amused by the aptness of the symbol his mind had selected.

Mariana would never love him like that. He did

not want her to scrub floors for him, but he wished that he could believe that she wanted to. He looked at her. Her face in the light of the street lamps was delicate and aloof. And suddenly the events of the evening, his memories of Mary Moore, were as nothing, as less than nothing to him. Now, as he looked at her, he only wanted to get home, to go to bed with her, to take off his clothes and make her take off even her thin, silk night-gown. To caress her so intimately, to have her so completely that he would be reassured, would feel at last that she was entirely his, part of him, while their bodies lay locked together in their final embrace.

Mariana was often physically exhausted from this constant excitation of her body. Sometimes she responded with delight to his embraces, and shared his ecstasy, more often she was too tired to be happy with him. But he throve strangely on love. He grew stronger, gayer. This room where Mariana waited for him was a secret tower to him, lovely as Rapunzel's.

Then when June came and the city was hot and breathless he grew tired. For ten years he had not had a holiday of any length and had not been out of the city for two years. He went more and more reluctantly to the newspaper office. The blinding lights made his head ache, the noise around him confused his jangled nerves. Mariana saw how dispirited he seemed and decided that he must have a long vacation in the country. She had her own small income, he could probably earn a little by special articles. They decided to go to Edgewood in the Catskills, because Mariana knew of a tiny cottage in the woods at the edge of a cliff which they could rent for almost nothing.

Alan resigned his position on the newspaper and gave up his room, moving his books over to Mariana's apartment which Sigrid was going to sub-let. They spent an afternoon carrying them over, a dozen or two at a time. Davenant met them at the corner of the street, laughing and flushed, their arms full of books, and stayed to help. The three of them carried hundreds of books up the three flights of stairs to her room, where they stood in horror and amusement watching the growing piles for which there were no place.

"You must do as de Gourmont did," said Davenant sententiously. "Move out when the books become too much for you and leave them the apartments."

Mariana was always pleased and amused by Davenant. He was so intelligent and so erudite, and so strangely unknowing and inexperienced. He read Freud and Jung to discover what human beings around him were like, and did not find it a very successful method. He talked very well on psychology, was qualified to teach it in a University : but he had no idea why his charwoman remained with her silly drunken husband or why young girls giggled together in the street. Human behaviour remained a mystery to him. But he was kind in his way as well as learned.

The books arranged as well as possible, they sat down to tea, and began to talk idly about women.

" I am always sorry for women," Davenant said. " Nature has given them so many disadvantages of which men take advantage. Cards are always stacked against them, dice weighted to fall in their disfavour."

He looked at Mariana as he spoke, and she was half aware of something pitying in his look as if he apprehended what the future might bring forth for her.

" Most women are mean worldlings who know very well what they want and will do anything to get it," Alan said combatively.

" It is possible to pity the sufferings even of an attic rat," Davenant replied. " And I think that on the whole women are rather better than men. They are on the average less cruel, I believe."

"They are cruel enough to each other," Alan said.

" Because they are in a doubtful and difficult

position. Magnanimity is a quality which flows most easily from full-fed, contented lives. There are many good qualities that only safe and well-fed people can *afford* to have. ' Ragged and dangerous ' is an old saying."

" Why do you talk of men and women as if they were separate species in nature ? " Mariana asked. " As if they were as different as leopards and armadilloes. They both belong to the order Man. Surely their likeness must be much greater than their difference."

" But it is their difference that is important," said Alan, smiling at her. He was not interested in her argument, but her words had brought her body before his eyes, and he wished that Davenant would go so that he could make love to her.

*　　*　　*

A day or two later Alan and Mariana took a little river steamer up the Hudson to Kingston. It was a small cargo boat, and stopped at every tiny settlement to take on freight, but they enjoyed this slow progression. The boat wandered from side to side of the river, sometimes tying up at the right bank to take on two barrels, sometimes at the left for three boxes and a crate of cabbages.

They sat on deck in the chill twilight. Tiny twinkling lights glittered like glowworms here and there along the shore. After they had watched them for a little while Alan wanted to go to bed.

It gave Mariana a curious pleasure to be with her lover in the tiny cabin. It pleased her to have Alan take her in his arms here. It was so secret in the small closed space, surrounded by lapping waves. Overhead she heard the voices of the workmen and the sound of casks rolled into the hold. But closely and secretly with the world shut out, they were lying in each other's arms. They might have been going anywhere, on the wildest adventures, up the Volga, up the Amazon, bound for Cathay, while the boat steamed slowly up the river. They lay still now and Alan was asleep, still holding her fast. She heard the waves lapping against the cabin side. They turned into the waves of the sea. She was on the prow of a great boat, bound for some unknown place. It was driving straight towards the rising sun.

They woke in the chilly dawn. A negro steward was knocking at the door and telling them that the boat had tied up at the dock and that they must get up if they wanted to catch the little narrow-gauge train that came to take the freight to various small towns. They dressed hurriedly. Passengers were so rare that there was no one to

88

carry their luggage, but Alan persuaded a sailor
to bring it on a hand truck. When they were in
the little train, Alan disappeared. Mariana was
alarmed ; the toy engine was blowing impatiently.
But he reappeared in a few minutes with their
thermos bottle refilled with hot coffee and some
thick, ham sandwiches. As the train meandered
through the mountain gaps they ate the sandwiches and drank the coffee. They were chilly
but happy. " Do you know Richard Middleton's
poems ? " asked Alan.

" No," said Mariana surprised. " I never knew
he wrote poetry. I've read ' The Ghost Ship.' "

" There's one I was thinking of last night just
before I went to sleep—one that begins :

> *Under the arch of summer*
> *The great, black ships go by*——"

" How charming that is—' Under the arch of
summer.' What a serene opening."

" Yes, but the poem isn't serene."

" Did he really kill himself because he was unappreciated ? He was so young. He might have
waited."

" I have heard he killed himself because he was
seriously ill."

They drank the last of the coffee. A lovely blue
haze was lifting from the mountains. Others had

died unhappy. They were alive. They were young.

The small cabin where they were to live until the autumn cold made it uninhabitable, was perched on the edge of a cliff in thick woods. There was only one room in which to read, to sleep, to make love, but a porch as large as the house itself had been built on in front of it with benches around the sides. This was to be dining-room, kitchen and bathroom.

The woods were full of chipmunks and squirrels. The chipmunks would sit on stones in the sun-light, coming as near as they dared to chatter and criticise. The squirrels fought in the tops of the trees. They dropped nuts on the roof and raced scolding across it in the dawn. The house was be-leagured by small wild animals. Skunks prowled about it all night. Frogs hopped in through the open door. When it rained, it rained in upon them : when the sun shone, it shone through chinks in the wall : it was like living in a hole in a tree.

At first the weather was fearful. A perpetual rain made it impossible to go out. They lived on tinned foods, bread and condensed milk till they found that a farm a mile away would supply them with milk and eggs and also with cabbages and tomatoes. But they were happy in spite of the rain. It was cold and they built smoky little fires in the wet chimney. Lying together on the bed in the rainy night they read until sleep or love overcame them and they slept long and deeply, lulled by the monotonous dripping of the rain from the boughs.

After ten days the weather suddenly cleared. The sun was hot and bright and the leaves and grasses shone and glittered wet and clean from the long rains.

Mariana found a friend. A large red hound which lived at the farm had taken to following her home when she went for milk. Soon he lived with them and only went home occasionally for meals. The people at the farm had never taken the trouble to give him a name : he was a young dog and they vaguely called him ' the puppy.' Alan was struck by his appearance of sad, unintelligent nobility and called him ' Hector.' Mariana liked this name because she remembered a line from an old ballad :

> *I gae you a steed was good in need*
> *An' a saddle o' royal bone,*
> *A leash o' hounds o' ae litter*
> *An' Hector calléd one.*

So he was always Hector to them and soon came to know his name. Mariana played with him and teased him and took him with her everywhere she went. He became passionately attached to her, and only a little less so to Alan.

Their relations with human beings were not so satisfactory. There were a number of artists who lived in the neighbouring country. Some of them Mariana knew already, and others she did not know called on them.

But Alan was unreasonably jealous. He was first angry that Mariana seemed so glad to see them and thought she could not be content with him alone, she wanted other people. And then in some queer, childish part of his nature he was jealous of her, jealous of her charm, of the special affections some of these people had for her. He knew he was attractive, and he had been much loved, and yet these people were not really interested in him ; they were interested in Mariana. He felt he was of no importance to them, except as Mariana's husband. His pride was obscurely wounded.

He became surly and untrustworthy in company. Mariana could never tell how he would receive people. Sometimes he was really rude. Mariana was distressed and gave up trying to entertain or go out except with the people she knew best, or those whom Alan seemed to prefer.

She was sorry that Alan was so difficult, because it made her relations with people uncomfortable. She was always trying to make the best of Alan's

sullen behaviour or afraid that he would be rude
again, so that when visitors were present she became anxious and self-conscious, and even when
Alan was not there the thought of his disapproval
laid a weight on her spirits. She thought that it
would be better not to see people at all than to
have these strained relations with them. After all,
her real life was her life with Alan. She would
make the best of that. But there was a difficulty
there too, for she realised that Alan really craved
society and would not be happy in this isolation.
He demanded some homage from the world that
it would not give him, except under rare and
special circumstances. Mariana could not force
the world to pay him this deference. She felt sometimes as if she had a child, but could not give it
the toys its fancy craved. And she herself, the very
nature of her personality, so attractive to many of
these artists, would help to deprive him of the
glamour that was necessary to his illusion. Already
Mariana realised this, while Alan only dimly felt
that something was wrong. Since his marriage he
had been less happy with other people. But he
was so happy alone with Mariana that as yet it
did not seem to matter a great deal.

They lived very much to themselves ; but they
were very happy. Alan when he was alone with
Mariana was almost always sunny and gay. He

spent these holidays chiefly in reading and lying in the sun. Then while the moon rose he would lie on the bench in the porch drawing plaintive sweet airs from his flute. ' Alan Water ' flowed from between his fingers, liquid and lovely on the night air. ' Robin Adair ' rippled like the wind blowing among the boughs. Or he would sing in a voice perfectly untrained but very pleasant :

> " *Oh Shenandoah, I love your daughter.*
> *Away you rolling river !*
> *I'll take her 'cross yon rolling water.*
> *Ah ! ha ! we're bound to go*
> *'Cross the wide Missouri !* "

One night of many the hound, Hector, lay as usual with his head against Mariana's feet like the hound representing fidelity in ancient monuments. Mariana thinner now and often tired sat on the bench where Alan lay. She was half asleep, the music flowed by her head in a crystal stream. She had an odd fancy that the notes caught like tiny silver bubbles on the needles of the pine-trees above them.

The hound was asleep. Mariana was half awake dreaming in the broad moonlight—her thoughts floating away with the strain and caught back again and again by the new notes of the pipe. Alan was lost in his music during the playing of each air, but when he ceased for the moment to play, he wanted Mariana's praise, her attention. She kept rousing herself from this waking dream to give him this desired meed.

" Mariana, how does that verse of ' Barbara Allen ' go, the Tavern one ? "

> " *Oh dinna ye mind, young man,*" she said.
> " *When the red wine ye was spillin,*
> *Ye bade the toast go round and round*
> *And slighted Barbara Allen.*"

" What shall I play next ? "

" Sing me something instead. Sing me the ' Lowlands Low.' I never can quite remember the words of the part about the little cabin boy who ' bored two at twice, and some were playing cards and some were playing dice—when the water flowed in it dazzled in their eyes.' How fine ' dazzled in their eyes ' is ! "

He began to sing :

> " *A ship have I got in the North Countrie,*
> *And she goes by the name of The Golden Vanitie,*
> *But I fear she will be taken by a Spanish Galalie*
> *As she sails by the Lowlands low !* "

But she felt tired. She wished that for once she could lie alone, sleep deeply all night without waking.

95

" It's time to go to bed," said Alan at last and she obediently roused herself. The hound awakened by her movement shivered and groaned. Mariana called him to his mat just inside the door and covered him up. She turned down the covers of the bed and hurried to undress, hardly staying to brush out her heavy tangled hair. But quick as she was, Alan was before her and received her in desirous arms. She was tired ; she wished that his passion would complete itself so she could go to sleep. But against her will, her body became excited under his caresses : a nervous agitation racked her. When at last he was asleep, she lay trembling with nervousness. Then slowly her excitement left her, and she felt weary and depressed ; but she could not sleep. All night long she lay awake, thinking with closed eyes or watching the slowly changing patterns of moonlight on the wall and floor.

When dawn came, she was still awake. The red light upon the wall somehow comforted and refreshed her. Soon it would be time to get up. Soon everyone would be awake. The hound, who had been out by himself hunting rabbits in the moonlight, came in and saw that she was awake. He put his great head on the side of the bed and looked sadly in her face with speechless devotion. She slipped her hand under his soft muzzle, and he stood leaning his head in her hand breathing great sighs of love. At last Alan awoke and Mariana gladly got up to begin a new day.

After that night there were others when she could not sleep. She soon gave up attempting to sleep at these times. When she could no longer bear lying still and was afraid that the restless movements, which she could not absolutely control, would wake Alan, she would creep cautiously out of bed. She would rise very softly as soon as it was light, and put sandals on her bare feet and a cloak over her nightgown, very quietly not to disturb him. Hector asleep on his mat would wake and rise and follow her, and they would walk together in the fields.

The sweet chilly morning air would flow around her body. When she grew tired, she would sit on a stone wall to watch the rising sun, with Hector sitting as close to her as possible, leaning against her with his great head on her knee, his eyes closed in an ecstasy of content at being so near this mistress of his choice.

As morning drew on they would cease to shiver half pleasurably in the keen air. With the sunlight lying warm upon them they would sit leaning together watching the brightening day.

Mariana thought that Alan was getting restless.

She was afraid that he was growing tired of the monotonous life they led in the woods so much alone. His desire for her body did not lessen, but he was more often irritable over little things. Mariana was unused to house work. The little she had done in New York, the slight meals she had cooked for herself, the occasional steak she had broiled for a friend had scarcely prepared her for cooking three hearty meals a day and getting afternoon tea. She did not mind doing it. She instinctively believed that no trouble was too great to take for a lover with whom you live— cooking, scrubbing, lying awake at nights in frozen discomfort not to wake him : these were nothing to the simplicity of her nature. It was not the abandonment of a loving woman that she felt but an unconscious conviction that when you accept love and life you accept them completely. If they require your body for their use, you give it uncomplainingly, and give charity as well. She only wished she was more used to housework and did it better.

Alan took her patient devotion as a matter of course. Other women had done as much for him. He did not stop to think how much frailer Mariana was and how differently bred compared to the hardier women he had known. He even complained to her that she did not cook as Mary

Moore had done. He became sentimental over the way in which Mary had learned to cook for him, trying to spur Mariana to fresh efforts by these narrations. She looked at him with a real wonder, astonished that anyone should be so ignorant of the human mind as not to realise that such comparisons would offend her. It was not that she resented them—if you marry people with peculiar lacks you must accept them or leave them. But she was less resigned when Alan scolded her, going on and on tiresomely because she forgot to put in the salt or scorched the potatoes.

With a sort of scorn she thought, " It is not a serious affair if this man's steak is not cooked precisely as he likes it one day. I try to please him. I am willing to work for him. But I cannot be deeply moved because the butcher forgot to send and he has to eat a boiled egg instead of one fried with bacon. He can make me feel that it is my fault; but it is not my fault. And in my secret heart I don't care at all."

She looked at him with a sort of cool wonder when he complained at such length of such un-important things. " How can he take himself so heavily ? He is a young man. When the eggs are boiled too much he behaves like a retired colonel with a bad temper. How can he go on in that way ? "

Her life seemed to be a combination of a courtesan's and a maid of all work's ; worn with caresses one hour, she was scolded like a tiresome servant the next.

But there were still even now many mornings when Alan was charming. He woke gay and laughing. They talked sometimes for hours over the breakfast-table—talked till it was nearly time for Mariana to get lunch. Then in a moment he would turn into a harsh taskmaster complaining, nagging.

When he had reduced Mariana, worn out by the length of his complaints, to tears, he would be sorry—but he could not help himself. After an interval he would be irritated again, and commence scolding again. Hitherto Mariana had always been able to escape from people when they were disagreeable. But married to Alan, drawn to him by physical and emotional ties, what could she do ? She felt as if Alan, holding her to him, had struck her in the face.

And as the days went on Mariana found herself sometimes fighting back. She turned critical eyes upon his weaknesses and examined his pretensions. When he attacked her she answered sometimes with angry scorn. Then she was sorry. She hated these contentions. She almost hated him at such moments for goading her into so ugly an attitude.

The autumn was almost over and they knew they could not stay much longer. The yellow leaves were falling, leaving the black boughs bare. A cold, winter wind hissed through the thin woods where so lately the leaves had been thick and green. The squirrels had disappeared. The chipmunks had hidden. Nearly all the birds were gone.

Mariana looked wistfully at the fallen leaves. She would have pinned them to the boughs, like some character in a story she remembered, to keep the winter away. It was beginning to be really cold but they still had their meals outdoors, taking the table out into the sunlight between the scruboak trees in the clearing in front of the shack. They gathered sticks in the woods to burn in the little fireplace. At night they lay on the bed covered with a steamer rug while they read or Alan played on his flute. No night yet had passed without caresses. As soon as he felt Mariana's young body in the bed beside him, Alan felt the stirring of his senses. He would lay his hand on her breast, and turning towards him, she would see the intent look of desire on his face. He would begin to kiss her, his mouth lingering on her mouth till his lust overcame his dreamy, passionate mood and she lay beneath him while his body, with a deliberate slowness to draw out this pleasure, delighted in hers. Afterwards they would fall asleep, hand in hand, her head on Alan's breast, his arm around her. With his limbs still twined in hers, Mariana felt closed in, safe. These arms, these thin human arms could shut out the terror of the night. No grey fear could enter the ring made by this wall of flesh and blood. Alan by day might be a taskmaster, repressing her happiness, but on such nights he was a fortress against the dark.

In the beginning of November they left the little house in the woods. Mariana said good-bye to Hector the hound. He must go back to the farm. When the old Ford which took them to the boat started, he tried to follow ; but he had to give it up and stood in the road looking after his goddess whom he might not see again. Mariana's eyes were full of tears, Alan was sad. It was the end of their summer. The little boat which had brought them up the river took them back to New York.

They had been talking for some time of going to London to live. Alan hardly remembered England and longed to see it again. Invested with memories of childhood and ideas of romance it had become his earthly paradise. Everything he disliked in the world was ' un-English ' : everything English was right. Mariana thought it might be better for him to return since these feelings made it unlikely that he would ever be really happy in America. She did not realise how early he had come away, and how much his England was a country of his imagination.

She thought, moreover, that their life together might be easier in a country where they would know no one, and would make their friends together, since Alan's resentment of her friends and peculiar disapproval of his own made life increasingly difficult. By living so cheaply in the mountains they had saved something towards the steamship fare. Alan was an experienced journalist who could find work in any English-speaking country. Mariana's small income would save them from actual want. They decided to go.

On a dark day in December they stood looking down from the high steep side of the steamer that was to take them away. They were watching for Mary Moore and Davenant who had promised to come to see them off.

Mariana could feel neither regret nor gladness. She was depressed by her own indifference among the kisses and ejaculations around her and by the look of the dirty water below full of straw and lemon skins, slapping against the ship and the piles with a cold, meaningless iteration.

From an unexpected direction Mary and

103

Davenant appeared together, Mary looking very beautiful in a torn black coat with an inch of petticoat hanging below it, for she and Shearn were both out of work, and as they never saved anything Mary had already pawned her best clothes. Yet she had brought presents of flowers and fruit.

Davenant also had brought Alan a book of Yeats' plays for masked dancers, and Mariana a translation of Lucretius. She was sorry to say good-bye to him. In the short time she had known him she had come to value his reserved limited friendship, and, ignorant herself, to appreciate his really remarkable erudition. Few of the people she knew would have realised that she would like to read Lucretius on the *Nature of Things*. In her rather adolescent world they were reading Aldous Huxley and Oswald Spengler.

The steamer blew a loud blast on her siren and the confusion of good-byes, of shouts and kisses, increased and died, Mary and Davenant hurrying away with the rest. They saw the upturned faces grow distant and unrecognisable as the steamer drew away from the dock. Small tugs like inquisitive fishes pushed with their noses at her prow and stern, directing her tremendous idle bulk with their insistent buffetings. At last in the full stream of the North river she floated between ferry boats and river steamers down the road to the sea. The towers of lower New York appeared, tall and alien to the sight as the palaces of some imaginary city ; they disappeared again in mist and darkness as if the city like Ys had been engulfed.

Then after all the steamer could not leave the harbour on account of the fog, and lay off quarantine all night blowing a loud melancholy horn at rhythmical intervals. Mariana lay listening to it and could not sleep. It was menacing, warning of danger. Her secret distrust of life with Alan was awake, roused by the loud blowing of the horn.

She thought, turning restlessly in her berth, that she must make the best of her future. She was young and strong and had made her bed herself. But she felt already that this journey was in vain : for they were taking with them their uneasy relationship, the root of all the difficulty. And though she left no family behind she felt as if she were leaving home. She was at least leaving something she knew for the unknown, and consequently the alarming.

When finally she fell asleep the horn blew through the thin walls of her dreams. It was warning a Roman city to rise—Hannibal was at hand : Roland was blowing his horn and no one heard.

Her dreams became more and more troubled. She was shipwrecked and tried to swim to land. But the waves before her grew higher and higher until she could no longer see the shore. She toiled up wave after wave, and the shore receded further and further, and still she struggled on. She was glad to wake in daylight to hear the steward knocking at the door with morning tea. But it was strange to find the dark dream-reality that surrounded her dispersed so easily by sound and light.

Alan woke gay and hopeful, pleased to hear English voices around him : he dressed hurriedly and went up to breakfast. But Mariana, tired with packing, stayed in her berth and had coffee and grape-fruit there.

She lay all day listening to the wind rushing by the port-hole and watching the dark blue water change, as the ship rolled, to clear blue sky. She was careless and indifferent, and happy with a sort of vegetable happiness, as a wild daisy perhaps is happy on a bright day, simply aware of sun and water and air.

The next day she rather regretfully got up and sat on deck in the sun with Alan. It was strangely warm for December, as if they had sailed out of winter into spring.

There were only a few people on board, chiefly

young Englishmen going home for Christmas.
The captain, to amuse them and possibly himself
—for he was a gay old sailor with a white beard—
gave dances down below every evening and tea
dances every afternoon on deck. Alan did not
care much about dancing but rather liked the
music and air of gaiety. And Mariana enjoyed it
all very much.

She was amused to find that as soon as these
young men discovered that she was married they
were disappointed and lost interest in her. She
had never wanted to flirt. She did not even understand how, having some peculiar lack of awareness
of her relation to men which her gradual awaken-
ing to sexual feeling had not affected. So that she
did not really mind that her marriage made her
less desirable ; but she was ironically amused to
find that it was so, and abstractedly sorry for their
obvious disappointment. Surely, she thought,
young women should not be so branded and put
aside that henceforth only one man should have
even a pleasurable sensation from their nearness
without feeling himself astray and on dangerous
ground.

The sight of Mariana in the arms of some young
man, swaying with him to the dance and the music,
always excited Alan. And later when they were
alone in their stateroom, closed in together with

the wind crying and the sea outside pouring by, he would throw all the blankets from the berths on to the floor and lie upon them with her. They would lie without moving and let the sea make love with them, rocking them together, swaying them apart and together again as if they were drowned in a sea of love.

The week's voyage was soon past. Mariana felt that an interlude of security was over. On this last evening they quarrelled while they were dancing, and she went downstairs to read in her berth. She fell asleep and was waked by Alan undressing her. He was in one of his rare tender moods—not undressing her to have her naked but so that she could slip quickly into bed. But by the time she was undressed his mood had changed and he was bent upon making love. She was sleepy and took no pleasure in his embrace ; but it left her restless. When she finally slept she kept starting awake, troubled with some undefined anxiety.

She dreamed, and dreamed always of looking for something which she could not find : and, sinking into a deeper sleep, seemed to awake wandering in the heart of a tropical jungle. The creepers and lianas were thick as snares. She pulled them apart only to find others behind them, and tearing those away from the branches

108

to which they grew found more and more beyond.
She saw a pagoda across the forest spaces. Its tiny
golden bells were ringing on the wind. She longed
to reach it. But the lianas grew thicker and thicker.
Her sleep became deeper : the forest and the
pagoda disappeared.

PART II

PART II

The day dawned cold and gloomy and a clammy mist wrapped itself about the ship. She docked at Southampton early on a raw, foggy afternoon. They could see nothing of the country. To Mariana it seemed that she had left one unsubstantial shore for another. But as the boat train travelled to London, they ran out of the fog into a clear, grey afternoon. The little villages stood in silver clouds where the smoke from the chimneys was caught and held in the wet air. Mariana was enchanted. It seemed as if each little town had its own atmosphere, separating it from the rest of the country. The stone barns built around square courtyards were strange and beautiful to her.

When they came into Waterloo, it was night. The small lights of London glittered and glowed around them. They rejected the taxis offered them and found a shabby four-wheeler. A frail old man made an effort to help them with their bag and Alan gave him sixpence. He was the first of the pathetic army of the out of work that they came to know so well in after-war London.

The four-wheeler rolled on and on upon its

way to the small hotel they had selected. Alan and Mariana sat in it hand in hand, excited but somehow disappointed. They could only see a confusion of changing streets of lights approaching and receding. The loud clop-clop of the horse's feet sounded in their ears. This was London. They could not feel quite what they wanted to feel.

At last they stopped at the door of an hotel near Hyde Park Corner.

When they had washed and settled their things a little, they went out to get something to eat, for dinner at the hotel was over. They did not know where to go and wandered by shops full of Christmas books and toys with streaming tinsel. Finally, they found an A.B.C. restaurant. They sat at a melancholy, brown marble table and ordered something uninteresting. The restaurant was nearly as cold as the streets outside and Mariana shivered in her rather thin coat. She felt tired and stiff with cold. She could not be gay. Her lips seemed carved in other lines when she tried to smile, and Alan was gloomy. But food and hot coffee revived them and when they left the restaurant it was better. Alan looked at the odder faces and figures around him with amused pleasure. It was plain that he saw it as a sort of coloured illustration out of Dickens.

Very tired they went back to the hotel and undressed rapidly in the cold room. There were two
narrow beds. Mariana and Alan each took one.
He did not come to her bed. It was the first night
that he had failed to embrace her, and while she
was tired and wanted to lie still, this first neglect
added to her feeling of loneliness and depression.
She heard the roar of the many-peopled city outside, and it frightened her. She lay feeling profoundly alone.

London depressed Mariana. The dark and dirty
air veiled the sun's light. She wanted to go about
and see the city, to visit St. Paul's and the Tower
and walk in the ancient parts of the City. But
they had first to find inexpensive lodgings, and
for a week or more all their time was taken up
by the search.

They thought they would try to live in Chelsea,
because Alan liked the idea of living where so
many writers had lived before, and they looked
there for a studio or apartment. But they could
find nothing which they could afford. The studios
were either too expensive or had no living arrange-
ments ; the flats were much too expensive.

Chelsea itself pleased them. They walked on
the embankment when the lights were first lit, and
the misty London air drifted almost tangibly
around them. They saw Crosby Hall standing

untenanted behind hoardings, but still showing its proud white front among the darker, more modern buildings on the river.

They determined to live in Chelsea if possible. They bought newspapers and sought out the advertisers of lodgings in the district. They climbed many dusty, dreary flights of stairs. Over-dressed and over-painted fat women showed them over-furnished, airless rooms. Dreary, down-trodden women in rusty black showed them stuffy, shabby rooms. One of these said as a recommendation, " The letter carrier lived in these rooms till his wife died."

" I won't," said Mariana as the door closed behind them, " live in the rooms where the letter carrier's wife lived till she died." She was half amused and half horrified by the idea of living in these poor lodgings. In France it might have been amusing to live over the cobbler's shop or in rooms formerly tenanted by M. le facteur ; but they manage these things better in France, and the poor are better housekeepers.

One dark afternoon they looked at a large single room, the top floor of a carpenter's house. Alan liked it because it reminded him of an attic room he had once had in Chicago where he had been happy and he wanted to take it, but it was on a busy street corner in a poor district. Mariana looked out of the window. It was a grey day. Dust eddied about the street and a cold wind lifted a piece of torn newspaper from the pavement. Her heart contracted with fear. If I live here, she thought, I shall never escape. I shall become a drudge. No spirit could survive this street. She hurried Alan away.

They finally took a large room looking down on King's Road, the main thoroughfare of Chelsea. This situation was unfortunate because of the noise. The buses whizzed by all day, but with the windows shut they found it not unendurable and after midnight the buses and most of the other traffic ceased.

Mariana liked the house because it was kept by an intelligent young woman who had been a governess, and was rather nicely furnished and perfectly clean and had a bathroom. Their room had two large windows which looked out on the empty sky, for it was at the top of the house and the buildings on the opposite side of the street were lower. She grew fond of standing at the window looking down at the shops and the people passing by. There was a butcher's stall almost opposite, and the butcher owned a large, middle-aged white bull terrier—the kind of dog that Bill Sikes has in Cruikshank's illustrations for *Oliver Twist*. Alan noticed that the dog was locked out on Sunday mornings while the butcher and his family were at church or chapel. The dog could never understand why he was not let in, and would sit at the door barking and scratching at intervals until his owner returned. They learned to know the habits of the people who lived on the street and the ways of the beggars who haunted it, the street musicians, the sellers of matches and the pavement artists. It was Christmas. Mariana bought a cold chicken and a plum pudding. She heated the plum pudding and burned brandy on it, and this was their first Christmas dinner together. And Alan spent a long, dark afternoon in making love to Mariana, and they slept while the dark day turned to darker night and the street lamps came out one by one.

On Boxing Day Alan said they must go to a pantomime and that they must stand in line for the gallery, both because the gallery seats were cheapest and because it would be an amusing thing to do. They chose *Dick Whittington* and took up their positions in a long queue. Street entertainers came to amuse them, as they came most probably to amuse waiting crowds in Shakespeare's time. One youth juggled with three balls and stood on his head. He got a few pennies in his cap at the end and went off. An old broken-down man in dirty rags with the beginning of a grey beard on his cheeks appeared. With his battered hat in his hand and his old face under its thin thatch of white hairs twisted up to the cold London sky he began to sing ' D' ye ken John Peel ? '

This poor old pauper singing of the horses and hounds and the morning, the strength and beauty that he would never see again, perhaps had never seen in all his sixty or seventy years on earth, seemed to Mariana one of the saddest things she had seen. Defeated by life and time he stood in the cold begging for a few pennies to eke out the rest of his misery. His hoarse voice cried to Heaven for a million wrongs. The wrongs of all the poor, all the unfortunate were crying aloud in the street for men to hear : and no one heard. Mariana looking at the faces about her saw them amused or indifferent. Poverty, misery, old age, hunger, loneliness were things they had seen so often that their minds were almost indifferent to them. The sight of age begging its bread in the street was no more to them than the sparrows picking up crumbs in the park.

The old man took his few pennies and went away. He was succeeded by a dark, angry-looking man with a crooked face, who recited ' Gunga Din ' in a cockney whine, but with something fierce in his manner which fixed the attention. When he passed his hat very few pennies were thrown in it. Those who were willing to give at all had given already. He said that he must have more with such a wolfish air that he was almost frightening. Mariana felt that this was a man who had been or would be driven into the criminal class by the difficulties of his life : there was in his whole personality something desperate and dangerous.

They were glad when the queue began to move into the theatre and left him behind. They found places on the hard, wooden benches and watched their first pantomime with perfect enjoyment. It was a splendid one. *Dick Whittington* in his silken rags and obvious though gallant femininity was a charming ' principal boy.' His love was prettily golden-haired, and there was a masculine dame in the best traditions of pantomime comedy, rough and satisfying. The cat was also a comedy character, and although a little large for anything short of a tiger, behaved most cat-like and made quick work of the rats on the fantastic island. The bells on the road for London rang ' Turn again Dick Whittington,' and ' all went merry as a marriage bell.'

Mariana and Alan, who loved the theatre, were almost as happy as the children around them. They slipped out during the intermission and had tea at a nearby Lyons, eating their buns hurriedly

and gulping their tea down not to miss the curtain
for the second half. Afterwards they climbed on
top of a Chelsea bus at the corner of the Strand,
and as they rode away past the lions in Trafalgar
Square, discussed the merits of the pantomime.
They stopped at a fried fish shop in the King's
Road, for the restaurants were all closed for Boxing Day, and bought two sixpenny pieces of fish.
This price includes a quantity of potato chips and
vinegar if you wish it. They took the fish home
and ate it with the fragments of their chicken.
They were very happy that night.

A few days later Alan complained of a sore
swelling on his cheek. Mariana examined it and
found there was pus in it, and Alan admitted that
he had a bad tooth in that part of his mouth. She
consulted the intelligent landlady who gave her
the address of a dentist in Kensington, and Alan
went to see him. But the dentist did not inspire
confidence and Alan came away with the tooth
undrawn. Mariana felt a sort of desperation. The
obvious incapacity of the dentist, vague and un-
decided in his expensive office, exasperated her.
She got the address of a surgeon who lived in
King's Road and took Alan there. The surgeon
was a panel doctor, and his bare cold waiting-
room was full of shabby, uneasy patients who went
into the surgery nervously and unwillingly one by

one. As the door closed behind one feeble-looking, ageing man, she heard the doctor's cheerful, careless voice say, " Well, how's the cough ? "

" This," she thought, " is one of the hours you have to pass through as best you may. There is nothing to be got from it, no interest, no enrichment of any sort. You live through it and feel it as little as you can. It is essentially evil and unfortunate. You are caught in it for an hour or longer, it may be. There is nothing to be done but live it out."

The last panel patient reappeared and Alan and Mariana went in. The surgeon, brisk but kind, examined Alan's face and mouth and said there was no question that the condition came from the tooth, but that it would be dangerous to have it drawn until the abscess was reduced ; then Alan must go to a particularly good Canadian dentist whom he knew. Mariana must poultice the cheek with linseed poultices to bring the abscess to a head.

Late that night and for several days and nights after, she sat by the fire and heated poultices for Alan's face. The sweetish, sickly smell of the linseed, such an old wives' remedy, brought all sorts of past associations to her mind. It had been a favourite remedy of her grandmother's and of all the darkie Maumas in the South. Alan was very patient and amiable during his uncomfortable illness. At night he would lie down and drowse and Mariana would fall half asleep over the saucepan on the hob and almost wonder in the light from the fire who she was and who was lying ill on the bed.

After a few days the surgeon lanced Alan's cheek, and told Mariana to continue the poulticing with hot boracic lint.

It amazed her that not an hour after this slight but quite painful operation, Alan must needs stop her poulticing to make love to her. She realised that the needs of the body and its stimulants are not quite what we suppose.

Soon he was well enough to have his tooth drawn, and after that recovered rapidly, pleased that his fine skin healed with hardly any scar.

Mariana felt depressed by their friendless state. If she had been very much in love with Alan and of a jealous nature, she might have been glad to have him alone in a foreign country, entirely hers, not shared with friends or relatives. But she was not particularly jealous nor sufficiently in love with Alan to feel this. She was alone among strangers with a stranger. Their natures were still alien for all their nights of love.

Alan went to see the editors of various newspapers and journals and took articles with him

or suggested them on the spot. He sold several
and had several orders. The fact that he could
place his work in England pleased and encouraged
him. But he was not really happy in London. He
was very British, but not English. He felt as if
he wandered in a book. He loved the characters,
but could not quite talk to them. He was outside
the pages. And the dark, murky weather of one
of London's worst winters depressed him, who so
loved sunlight and warmth. Day after day the
sky was heavy and overcast. There was a dull,
yellow fog that could be tasted, that choked the
lungs and got in the eyes ; or at best the sun rose,
a dim yellow disk, and its pale chilly light streamed
through the dirty air and lit the shabby streets
around them.

Alan became depressed and irritable. He
nagged Mariana for an hour at a time because
she forgot to put the salt-cellar on the table or to
buy vinegar for the beetroot. At other moments
he could be very charming. Curiously enough he
did not care to see the ancient buildings and his-
toric places of the country he so much loved. He
was content simply to live in it. He found end-
less interest in the moving life of the streets. He
loved to go to the public houses in the poorer
quarters of Chelsea and on its edges. He would
sit listening to the talk that went on around him,

drinking his glass of beer, or discuss with the men the merits of different prize-fighters or different kinds of dogs. He found an extraordinary pleasure in these small encounters and he would amuse Mariana for hours with descriptions of little things he had seen in his solitary rambles around London. He did not take Mariana with him on these walks, partly because of her sex. A young girl, and moreover a very unusual-looking girl, attracted too much attention. He could not go with her into the bar of a pub and listen unnoticed to the talk around him. Nor did he like to take Mariana to Whitechapel or Limehouse ; it would hardly have been possible except with a party, and he could never tell beforehand where his rambles would take him, what odd corner he would discover.

Then he was glad to be away from her for part of the day. They were so close together most of the day and night. Their very emotional situations made it difficult for them to be so constantly with one another. Often their love-making left a current of irritation behind it.

Mariana recognised all this and still she wished that Alan would take her with him. She did not go very far by herself, for she had developed a particular fear of London. She had not lived long enough in New York to grow used to great cities and London seemed much more formidable. The damp cold, the darkness, the maddening traffic frightened her. She saw a man killed by a lorry soon after they came. Then Alan's sudden illness alarmed her. It seemed to her that anything might happen in such a place—Alan might die and leave her alone, or she might die here among strangers. And when she thought of that Alan seemed a stranger too.

But on clear days she would sometimes walk from Chelsea all the way to Trafalgar Square and visit the National Gallery or the National Portrait Gallery where she bent her head over the death mask of Keats or looked up wonderingly into the mad ecstatic gaze of the beautiful face of John Clare, the poor poet who lived his life half as a farm labourer and half in a madhouse, who was so many years insane that when he returned to his home, people thought he must be a ghost— and so he was in all but being dead.

Gradually they came to know a few people. Alan met in the office of one of the weeklies a young Scottish writer, Donald McLeod. One night when Alan and Mariana went as an un-usual treat to one of the Chelsea restaurants, ' Ye Olde Ship,' or some such place, they met McLeod there and Alan introduced him to Mari-ana. She liked him at once. He was slight with dark hair and his whole appearance was sensitive and intellectual. But his warm vigorous pressure when he shook hands and a certain strength and dignity which she felt in his personality, for all his youth and look of physical delicacy, interested and attracted her.

He asked them to come to tea and they found that he lived near them in Chelsea. It was the first time that Mariana had been out to tea in London. McLeod was the first person that she had met at all since her arrival. She decided to put on her favourite dress. It was an odd, pretty dress of brown velvet, trimmed with broad bands of brown fur. She wore it because its fur matched the short, fur jacket in which she had been married, and to go with it she had a wide-brimmed hat of flame-coloured velvet faced with brown chiffon. Her whole appearance, dressed in this odd, rich costume of fur and velvet was so strange and mediæval that Alan was delighted. He never thought her beautiful as painters did ; she could not tease him into saying that she was even pretty. And the fact that he did not think her really good-looking always amused her greatly. Secretly she agreed with him. She thought that the painters and the others who had admired her had very odd taste. When she looked in the glass she saw what seemed to her a thin young creature

127

with wide grey eyes and dark curled hair. She herself preferred girls to have golden hair and pink cheeks or best of all red hair and the lovely apple blossom colouring that sometimes goes with it.

But she liked to tease Alan for thinking her plain. In fact he did not think her plain at all. He thought her body beautiful with all its human flaws and imperfections—admired, even apart from the lust they evoked in him, her round breasts and strong, round thighs. But he did not think her pretty. He said she had a strange charm of her own. To-day he thought she looked more like a sister of Gainsborough's 'Blue Boy' than a living girl walking in the streets of Chelsea. He looked at her with abstract admiration and surprise, and said, " That costume certainly suits you."

Amused by his stiff phrase she gave him a sidelong look from her slanting grey eyes and began to laugh. He thought there is something positively elfish about Mariana. I cannot believe she is quite like other people. And he was not pleased with his idea, for after all, he thought, in a wife a man wants a girl of flesh and blood, a woman who loves him and who can cook and keep a house. He doesn't want an inhuman creature who has thoughts stranger than his own. The idea flickered not through his conscious mind, but through its vaguer depths. It was a thought that had appeared there before—a dissatisfaction with Mariana, a realisation that she did not love him as he felt she should, as indeed he knew he could be loved for he had been so loved. Somewhere there had been a mistake. He could not make Mariana really his. She escaped him always. When he scolded her, grew angry with her, he could make her cry—but those tears were not tribute to him. It was not because he scolded her that she cried, not because her loved lord was angry with her. It was because this world in which she found herself was sad. They were tears of regret she shed for some other order of existence from which she had somehow been exiled, which she could not recover again. A gust of real anger stirred his mind. She must be *neurotic*. Other women had been content with him. It was her fault.

They were at Donald McLeod's door and his mood was broken by the need for ringing the bell and announcing themselves. McLeod had charming rooms. The fire in the grate was shining and tea came in on a great tray bright with silver and painted china. The window of the room in which they sat looked out on an extraordinary building, an imitation Gothic castle covered with all sorts of odd pieces of bad sculpture stuck here and there in niches provided for the purpose. Mariana saw a battered bust of Queen Victoria and another of the Prince Consort. Next to them was a copy of a fat Roman cupid, and beyond that she noticed a worn saint and a head, she thought, of Voltaire.

" That's old Mr. Ferney's house," said McLeod. " Isn't it amazing ? " It was evidently one of the sights of Chelsea. " I'm afraid they are going to tear it down," he added.

" Is he dead ? " asked Mariana.

" Yes," said McLeod, " he died some years ago, but they left the house as it was. He went mad apparently after the death of his wife with whom he was very much in love. He thought that he came of an old French family, which may have been true, but he imagined that the family had had a Gothic castle in France and that all these pieces of sculpture came from it, though he really picked them up second-hand himself. He was one of those amazing eccentrics you find at their best only in England. " Will you pour the tea, Mrs. Douglas ? " he continued.

" But I've forgotten how to pour tea properly," she answered half seriously. " I have a cracked brown teapot and two cups, and I burn toast at the grate."

After that they saw McLeod quite often.

Sometimes he came to tea with them, and did not appear to notice the deficiencies of the service. She toasted scones for him over the fire, and with the cold, dark afternoon shut out behind the curtains, the room lit by fire and lamp-light seemed very cheerful on the days when he came. It made a great difference in her feeling about London. It did not seem so alarming a place after all since there was someone in it who was friendly to her.

Alan made several other acquaintances among the men with whom he came in contact in Fleet Street and Chelsea. But Mariana seldom met them, for Alan did not want to take her with him to the houses where he went. He did not like to go about with a wife. It made him, he felt, a less romantic figure.

Mariana both sympathised with and despised his attitude. She was ashamed of the feeling of scorn she sometimes had for him. She thought then that there was some essential inferiority in this attempt to escape maturity and responsibility. She felt that she was being rejected by an inferior —and was ashamed of her feeling.

The nervous difficulties of her life with Alan affected her more and more.

She often did not sleep well, and grew thinner and more tired as the winter went on. Alan's

embraces, even when she took pleasure in them.
left her jaded and weary ; once or twice she began
to cry quietly to herself and could not stop for a
long time. On one of these occasions Alan took
her in his arms as he lay on the bed beside her
and tried to comfort her. From comforting he
passed to embracing her, but she continued silently
and without change of expression to weep. She
had such an impression of woe that she hardly
noticed his embraces. Her tears were wet as rain
on his face. Embracing the mourning girl gave
him a strange pleasure as if he embraced sorrow
itself.

Then one day her chest began to ache as she
breathed. It continued all day, and she began to
think that she had pleurisy. Sitting after tea on the
floor by the fire, she told Alan how her chest
ached and turned her tired head to lay it against
his knee. It was a melancholy and hopeless gesture,
as a dying man might turn his face to the wall,
and it profoundly saddened Alan. He laid his
thin hand on her head and said sadly, "My poor,
brown elf." He hardly knew what to do—he had
come to rely so much on Mariana, and now she
might be dependent on him. The idea of her being
ill under these conditions depressed and bored him.
He thought he had better take her to a doctor,
tried to say so with cheerful decision and brought

her coat and hat, as it was the evening office hour of the doctor whom they had visited before.

Again they waited in the dreary waiting-room and watched the unhealthy panel patients go in unhappily one by one. Alan felt depressed and angry at this stream of human pain in which he and Mariana were caught to-night. She had sometimes told him that he was a devil worshipper, that he would not believe in God, but would believe in the Devil and see his work in the world. Here, he thought, is work of the Devil. No good creator could have made these poor creatures and set them in misery. Why should Mariana's chest be aching? It could as easily be well. If there is any power abroad to-night, it is a power of evil.

Finally they went into the surgery. Mariana had to take off her clothes down to the waist. She was a little embarrassed so to undress before Alan— and Alan was embarrassed also to have her stand naked before him for the first time, with a strange man beside them. The doctor examined her chest carefully and said he was almost sure she had not got pleurisy. He could not hear the characteristic ' new leather ' creak at all. What she had was neuritis. She was too thin. She should try to gain, cover up the nerves, improve her general health, keep warm and dry. He'd give her a sedative and a tonic, and she'd be all right. There was really nothing the matter.

They left. Mariana, pleased that she didn't have pleurisy, felt a wave of relief. The pain in her chest seemed better already. They had the prescription made up, and Alan asked for a glass and gave her a dose of the sedative at once. He was greatly relieved that she was not going to be ill on his hands. He decided that a cinema would divert her and do her good ; so they went into the first one they came to and bought eightpenny tickets.

It was a very cheap, shabby cinema, and crowded with small boys. They were waiting with restive excitement for the picture to begin, shuffling their feet, giggling and laughing, snuffling and coughing and pushing each other about. Alan, who disapproved of children on principle, though he often liked them and enjoyed playing with them in practice, spoke severely of their behaviour, but Mariana, who liked little boys, was diverted by them and wondered what the picture which they were expecting so eagerly would be.

At last the lights went down, and the excitement, the scuffling and snorting increased till it reached a supreme point as the first white flicker began, and then burst deafeningly into shrill cheers.

THE NIGHT RIDERS the glaring headlines

134

proclaimed. PART TWO. BUCK REVEL'S RIDE.
It was a serial *Western*.

The words disappeared suddenly into open air
with a solitary horseman coming over the crest of
a hill covered with sage bush. The shouting
ceased instantly, turning into an audible loud-
breathing silence.

Mariana and Alan also watched delighted. The
film was so old that it was dark and grained like
wood and foxed like an old print, and this increased its beauty, for the texture was that of a
worn engraving. The acting was terrible, the story
ridiculous, the photography bad, the lighting
wretched ; but everything that made it poor as a
movie increased its beauty as a picture.

And oh, the relief of turning away from the
noise and smoke of London into this clear dark
air and these open silent plains.

Some lines from a poem she half remembered
came back into Mariana's mind. It was a poem,
she thought, about a sweat-shop worker, a girl
born and bred in the slums who goes to movies
to escape :

> *The tenement rooms are small,*
> *The walls press on the brain,*
> *But oh ! the lilt of the galloping horses*
> *Over the endless plain.*

Two riders galloped towards them over the crest of the hill. The effortless movement of the horses was like the running of water. The riders swung in their saddles to the swing of the horses' movements : every turn and twist balanced against another with a perfection of ease. Soundless, sweatless, effortless, the horses galloped through the evening air, and Mariana and Alan and the children watched them, released in another world free from the sweat and burden of reality.

*   *   *

Spring came at last though it was as cold and almost as dark as ever. They began to talk of the summer. They decided to leave London, to see the English country which they had never seen. Mariana thought Alan would want to go to Scotland since his father had come from Fifeshire, but his heart was set on seeing the West of England, going to Devon and Cornwall. He thought it would be warmer there, and after the cold, dark winter he longed for sun and warmth. They decided to go on a walking trip ; they would carry as little as possible and walk from village to village, spending their nights where they could find lodgings.

But it was the first of June before they left

136

London, taking an express to Taunton, which Alan chose because it was the first express stop in the country to which they wanted to go. Taunton turned out to be a bigger town than they had supposed. They had lunch at an inn near the station, and heard a burly farmer talking to the landlord about the price of cattle. They had left London. They were in another world.

A thin rain had begun to fall, and they put on their rain-coats before they adjusted their knapsacks. Alan looked at his map of the western counties and decided to walk to Norton Fitzwarren because it was only a few miles away and had an attractive name. They asked the landlord which road to take. " Norton ? " he said. " Go straight down the main road, turn off it to the right when you come to ' The Swan,' and that's your road. Norton," he expanded, " was a big town, a market town, a long time ago. There's an old proverb about it.

> *Norton was a busy town*
> *When Taunton was a vuzzy down.*"

" Was a what ? " asked Alan.

" Vuzzy is Somerset for furzy, covered with furze," the landlord explained, pleased that they had not understood.

They found later that this saying was current in every town in that part of England, and for all they knew, in every town in the country, with the names changed to fit. But it pleased them at the time as a bit of local lore, and they buttoned their coats at the neck and stepped out cheerfully into the wet. They passed through the streets and were out of the town in a short time. The world was wonderfully green. The grass was long and thick and they remembered that it was the first day of summer. A thin, silver rain was falling, but they thought it beautiful. The air was mild and still. They passed brown cows standing knee deep in grass. They stood by a stream which was flowing level with its banks, spilling over into the grass. And then they saw the may—trees of white may—and, caught and held in the crystal of the wet air, its dusky, summer scent. Mariana drew a deep breath. There was a feeling in her throat like tears.

It seemed to her as they walked down the country road in the soft rain under the boughs of may that they had left the sad, dreary world in which she had been imprisoned and had walked into the earthly paradise. It was too lovely to be possible. They had found some country between time and tears.

It was five o'clock when they reached Norton

Fitzwarren. They saw a Norman church, an inn called 'The Ring of Bells' and ten or twelve thatched cottages. At one of these, chosen at random, they knocked and asked if there was anyone in the village who would give them tea. The woman who opened the door said she could give them tea with eggs and lettuce. No, she had no rooms to let, and the inn had no rooms. But there was an old woman who had a big house across the street; she let rooms; the cobbler and the school-teacher lodged with her. Yes, she had several rooms. After a tea-supper they went to see the old woman, and she agreed to let them have a large room for the night at the price of half-a-crown.

They went through her flagged kitchen and climbed the stairs to see it. Alan said he wanted to go to 'The Ring of Bells' to listen to the company, so Mariana went off for a walk in the direction of the small church which she could see in the distance. She climbed a path that led to the top of a green hill. Below her she could see a solitary ploughman driving his furrow along a green slope. It was after seven o'clock, but this man still went to and fro behind his brown horse, bent over the handles of his plough. She wondered who he was, ploughing so late alone; what he thought of as he turned and re-turned in the air that was beginning to darken. She stood and watched his solitary form moving back and forth. Perhaps he watched her too as she climbed the slope. Their figures contained in this dark bowl of evening, unique in all years, may have remained for ever clear in their distinct far-separated minds—one creature watching another across the dark hill in the coming night and each wondering what life the other led, and what face a clearer sight would show.

It was growing dark when she returned and as she was undressing, Alan came in. He had been told at ' The Ring of Bells ' that there was a dance at the Village Hall lately built by the Squire. He had gone to see it, but had not found it very interesting. The conversation at the inn was better. He began trying to imitate the Somerset dialect.

There was a vast bedstead heaped high with a great feather bed and three steps at the side of the bed by which to climb to its downy eminence. And lost in its feathers, as if they slept on the breast of a goose, they lay deliciously warm and soft ; and in this bed they presently embraced and fell asleep, sunk fathoms deep in down.

The next morning they awoke early. The sun was shining. The old woman who kept the house brought them a tray with biscuits and tea which they managed to drink without spilling it among the feathers that billowed about them.

There was a hideously enlarged photograph of a policeman in full uniform over the bed. There were others about the room—two of children, and one of the policeman in his youth sitting stiffly in a chair with a girl in a wedding dress standing beside him. Before they left the house that morning they had heard from the withered old landlady that the policeman had been her husband and that dark young girl herself.

They had breakfast, coarse but filling, at the kitchen table while they talked to the old woman. Then they went out to see the country about them, turning down a narrow lane they left the little village behind.

It was June, but it seemed to Mariana like a day in spring, for all the trees were in bloom. There was a tree of dark, red may. She stood and looked at it in wonder. The colour, neither rose nor red, but dark and dusky and somehow like the bloom on fruit, resembled nothing she had seen or imagined. All the thrushes and blackbirds in the world were singing about them and the air was trembling with the ecstatic singing of the larks. They passed a cottage where two small, yellow-haired children sat in the grass playing with a striped, grey kitten and came to a stile, where trees of white may grew beside the lane. There they sat down on a bank.

Mariana was in a trance of wonder at this translation into beauty. She turned her face to Alan's and leaned against his breast. Something within her was singing and beating against the cage of her mind. Alan kissed her indulgently. But she knew he kissed Mariana, the girl who had shared his bed. It was not that kiss she wanted. She had wanted to share with him the strange rapture of the morning, but this he did not feel. He was happy because the sun shone, and the country was pretty, and it was English. He did not see the incredible beauty that she saw. She was in paradise alone.

They left the bank and wandered hand in hand up the hill towards the church. There they found the door open and went in and sat for a little on a red cushion in a dark pew, looking through the windows of clear glass at the clouds passing by outside, and then back to the altar covered with a red cloth worked in golden letters. They stopped in the entry as they went out to examine some framed scrolls which hung there. These were about the peals of bells rung in the church by the bell ringers on different occasions. They told the names of the ringers and the names and numbers of the peals rung—so many triple-bobs and triple-majors—the peals rung when King Edward was buried and on the day that King George was crowned. It pleased them to think of these bells ringing out over the tiny village, heard by few ears, sounding over the fields for the rabbits and the crows. They thought it must be because of these bells and their ringers that the village inn had been called ' The Ring of Bells.'

They had an early lunch and walked as far as Wellington, stopping for tea at a cottage. Their way led partly along the main road. It was a bare, tarred road and bungalows straggled along it.

Mariana began to flag. Her knapsack, light as it was, was too heavy for her shoulders. Alan took her knapsack as well as his own and strode ahead with them. His body for all its slightness was strong and sound. Years of cricket and rugby at school and then at his University had developed the naturally strong frame inherited from his vigorous, Scottish ancestors.

Mariana straightened her tired back and followed gratefully. They were walking in the green shadow of trees now, and Wellington was in sight. It turned out to be an ugly town, but they found a lodging with a pleasant old woman who lived in a small cottage hidden with its garden of cabbages behind a row of bigger houses. She had so many cats and dogs that they thought they never saw all of them, though grey cats and white dogs seemed to be lying in every room and hallway they passed, and there were more in the garden.

The next morning happened to be a market day, and on their way out of town they stopped at the open-air market to see the sheep and calves being sold. Some of the people who came amazed and delighted them. One wizened old man stood at the edge of the market, wearing gaiters and a jacket with small horseshoes instead of buttons. On his head he had a hat with a very high steepled crown—a hat the Pied Piper of Hamelin might have worn. He gave them a look of country cunning as they went by. "We amazed him too," Mariana thought with amusement.

They set out to walk into Devon. The old woman had given them an empty beer bottle, and Alan had it filled at an inn with the famous cider of Somerset. They stuffed their pockets with bread and cheese, and started off in high spirits. It was overcast, but no rain fell, and the green of the fields and the trees had a thousand delicate variations. Their way lay still along a high road, but they climbed up a bank and sat on the edge of a cornfield to eat their lunch. This simple food so eaten was like a sacrament. Bread and cheese and cider, immemorial food eaten once more by man and girl. How many haymakers, they thought, might have sat in this spot eating these very things? They lay in the grass resting and Alan went to sleep. Mariana watched the silvery gnats gathering over his head, then it began to rain gently; the first cold drops woke Alan and they went on their way.

All afternoon they walked along a small road that led between fields of green. It was deeply sunk between grassy banks and they came to no houses. They saw no one. They had not supposed it was possible to find so lonely a road in England. They almost thought that they had lost their way, except that any way was theirs in the country.

But presently they came to a single house. They knocked, hoping the woman would get them tea, but no one answered. A grey cat came around the corner of the house and arched its back, purring. A hen cackled. They knocked again, but no one came. "They have gone to market," said Mariana. They stroked the cat, who purred loudly at this attention and mewed, complaining that it had been left alone. Then they went on. They walked for miles, stopping sometimes to smell the pink campion or herb-robert. It was still raining a little, and the country had a lovely wet green look under the low grey sky. Suddenly, at the end of a field, they came to an inn. It stood so solitary in the empty fields that they could hardly believe it was an inn until they saw its swinging sign, ' The King's Arms.' The innkeeper had a quiet, almost sophisticated politeness. They thought he must have been a servant, a butler or valet who had saved money, but why had he taken ' The King's Arms ' in the midst of the empty fields ?

They took a room for the night, and after tea Mariana sat in the sunlight—for the sun was shining faintly between still threatening clouds—on a settle outside the inn door. A white road stretched away on either side. Before long three workmen appeared and went into the bar, and a two-wheeled cart drove up. The driver was accommodated with a glass of beer, brought to him where he sat, for he was afraid to leave his young horse. Then a boy arrived on a bicycle and had something to drink, and a man who might have been a schoolmaster tramped up with a knapsack on his back and was heard asking for a glass of stout and some bread and cheese.

There was something curious about all these people who appeared from nowhere, for not a house was to be seen. Mariana strained her eyes. She could not see even a wreath of smoke on the horizon. It was like an inn in a mystery story—a solitary inn where the conspirators were gathering in disguise.

146

After dinner they went for a walk. As they wandered in the twilight down the lanes whose banks and hedges were high above their heads, horses which they could not see leaned down to smell them and snorted at them like dragons. Mariana leaped in alarm as she felt the sudden gust of warm breath down her neck. They laughed and heard the heavy feet of cart horses moving away.

The primrose air of twilight enclosed them in a green darkening world. Faint airs sweet with unseen flowers blew about their heads. They met no one. They were in the fields alone. Slowly they wandered back to the inn and went to bed. There they lay curled in each other's arms, like wild creatures hidden in their cave ; Mariana felt herself sinking down into an intangible sea, and when it closed over her head, she found that it was sleep.

The next morning they awoke early and remembered that it was Sunday. They were impatient to be gone. They had decided to walk to Tiverton. When they asked the landlord the direction, " Keep the bells on your left," he said, " all the way, and you can't go wrong. Presently, you'll come to an old canal. Follow the tow path till you see a little village, then you'll be on the main road to Tiverton."

147

They set out and kept the bells on their left, as if the sound were a building in the air, and soon came to the canal. It was an old disused canal, full of green water-plants, and the banks were softly green. They walked along beside the water and still heard the ringing of the bells. Presently it began to rain and they took shelter under an old bridge. Through a thin curtain of falling drops, they watched a solitary angler who continued to sit holding his line in the rain. It was like a tailpiece from Bewick, Alan thought. As it continued to rain and there was no promise that it would ever stop, they decided to go on and walked for several miles along the old canal. Once they came to a little church. It seemed to be on the edge of a park and at a distance they could see a square, old house set among ancient oak trees.

They left it and walked on till they came to a village. There they discovered a bus going to Tiverton and took it. Tiverton, they were amused to find, was the town where Jan Ridd went to school. They looked at the buildings of the old Grammar School and Alan bought a sixpenny paper-backed copy of *Lorna Doone* to read on the spot.

They stayed for a few days in an old house on the edge of the town. It had a great square kitchen into which they once wandered by mistake. The woman who let the rooms was sitting sewing on a settle by the fire, her half-grown son sat on a stool mending the reel of a fishing-rod. The girl who waited on them was stirring batter and singing in a low voice. They were amazed to hear the words, for she sang :

" *A ship have I got in the North Countrie,*
  And she goes by the name of ' The Golden Vanitie.' "

The woman of the house asked them to sit down. " Where did you learn your song ? " asked Alan. He hoped she would say from her grandmother.

" At the school. They taught us old songs and dances."

" You know more, then. Will you sing another?"

" Oh, yes," she said cheerfully and began.

> *There was a rich merchant*
> *In London did dwell.*
> *He had but one daughter*
> *An uncommon fine young gel.*

It was one of Alan's favourites and he took out his flute and played a running accompaniment. They asked him to play something else, and he played a chanty—

One more day, my John, one more day—
Rock and roll me over one more day.

Then he paused a moment to remember, and
from his pipe flowed the notes that shape 'Robin
Adair,' the dancing sweet air, so light and so
wistful, which Handel said he would rather have
written than all his oratorios.

Mariana sat silent on the settle by the fire. The
whole scene was charming to her, the great
kitchen and the people in it at their work and
Alan playing his flute. The part of him that made
her love him, his boy's simplicity, shone in that
moment as clear as the glasses in the firelight.

They left Tiverton a day or two later to go to
Exeter. There it was some time before they could
find a lodging. They wandered up and down the
little back streets of the town envying the people
whom they saw comfortably at tea behind the
coarse lace curtains, always drawn tenderly
aside, but still softly enclosing the aspidistra in its
shiny green or pink pot—the ornament and shrine
of each respectable little house.

Mariana always felt a certain shyness about
going to ask for lodgings with Alan. It was showing
to the world her intimate connection with him.
It is no wonder, she thought in Exeter, as the
women who came to the doors seemed to refuse

them lodgings with narrow suspicious looks—it is no wonder they refuse to let us have a room for the night to make love in. They look at us with sharp, disapproving looks. They are quite right, we would make love in their cold beds.

Finally they found a gloomy, high house. A bitter-looking middle-aged woman kept it. They took the one room she had to let. As they sat at breakfast the next morning, she told them in her harsh voice that her last lodger had left after a week without paying his rent. She said she had never been married. " My sister married and what did it get her ? She's had four children and her husband's sick, and she goes out to work." There was an evil look of triumph in the wretched woman's face. The bitterness of her own hard and lonely lot seemed a little gilded by her sister's misery.

Alan thought her the most horrid creature he had ever seen. She quite spoiled Exeter for him. The beauty of the cathedral could not get her out of his mind.

The rain, too, discouraged them. " Let's take a train and go somewhere in Cornwall. Perhaps it will be sunnier and warmer there," said Alan. They looked at the map.

Mariana saw the name *Looe*. " Let's go there," she said. " It was the town next to Troy in *The*

Mayor of Troy. It was very nice in George III's reign, perhaps it still is."

They took a ticket to Liskeard and then changed to a tiny narrow-gauge train which ran a few miles further on to the sea. And when they reached Looe, the sun was shining !

They wandered from the new town across the bridge to the old town which clung to the steep sides of a low hill looking out to sea. There they found a lodging with one of the many Mrs. Penge-thorns of Looe. The next day the sun was still shining, and Alan said they would stay. They stayed for several months.

Mariana loved Cornwall. In her delight at being in the country again she was always outdoors in all weathers. She explored her surroundings, following every road or cart track to its source. One way led along the coast past Talland Sands where a half ruined church stared down at the shattered hull of a ship with dry black ribs projecting from the engulfing sand ; the road passed by it and passed by farms and fields till it came to Polperro, where gulls walked about the gardens like chickens and roosted on the chimney pots like starlings. Another road led inland to a hill where they sometimes went in the evenings hoping to hear nightingales, until they found out that nightingales are unknown so far west in England. But they heard other birds whose singing was wonderfully sweet.

" Missel thrush be better than nightingale," a man at ' The Jolly Sailor ' said to Alan as they sat one evening talking over their beer. They thought it might well be true.

There was a troupe of pierrots which played on the beach. They sometimes sat on the wall to watch them and threw pennies in the tambourine as it was passed among the crowd. The best of the pathetically bad performers was a dark young man who always wore the same suit with black and white lozenges. Mariana and Alan, with so little to occupy them, noticed him and called him the Black and White Pierrot. They noticed too that he always went about after hours with an old woman dressed in black with a black bonnet, like some character out of Dickens. He even took her to ' The Jolly Sailor,' where they could be seen through the window sitting comfortably in the inner parlour, and having something hot.

The Black and White Pierrot was attracted by Mariana's looks and by her cheerful applause of their most hopeless acts (she thought they needed it most), and tried to make friends with her and Alan. And Mariana was interested by him, and wanted to know more about him and find out how he lived, and what his relations with his old mother really were. But Alan who by himself particularly liked talking to vaudeville performers and also to circus freaks was more reserved when Mariana was with him : he did not think it was proper for her to make friends with strange pierrots on beaches and did not encourage the young man.

However, they went to his Benefit Performance (and even bought shilling tickets for the enclosure) before he returned to London, perhaps to take some little part in a play or on the music-halls, perhaps only because he could not make a living as a pierrot. They did not know.

Their landlady had one daughter, a young married woman, whose husband was a private in the army and had been sent to India three weeks after their marriage, while she had stayed at home.

She did not seem to feel the separation particularly, but wrote him a letter once a week and sent him her weekly copy of one of the more yellow Sunday journals.

" What can the man suppose the country is like ? " Alan said. " He must think by this time that the population consists of three drunken taxi-drivers, four confidence men and five half-witted chambermaids who are raped every week."

The girl seemed entirely dull and was not pretty, and they wondered why the soldier had ever thought of marrying her. And what they would think of each other after five years' separation.

" What do you do on winter evenings ? " Mariana asked the young woman one day. " Do you go to the moving pictures ? "

" No, there isn't any pictures in winter," said the young woman, and stopped.

" Are there dances or parties ? "

" No."

" Do you get books from the library ? "

" No, I never was one to care much about reading," the girl answered.

And Mariana decided that she was being neurotic to worry about the loneliness and boredom of the girl's empty evenings. After all, she thought, you would not ask a rabbit or a cow how it spends its evenings.

Mariana always now felt something essentially barren and dry in her life with Alan, though their days in Looe were pleasant enough. When all the household work was well done by other people there was little for Alan to scold about. In the brighter, warmer weather he regained his good humour. He made elaborate love to her on the white bed from which they could watch the sea.

In the kind air with less to trouble her, she improved wonderfully in health and spirits. Her solitary walks, for Alan seldom went with her, were really happy. But she felt it as an intermission in a hopeless defeat, as if she gathered flowers on the edge of a field in Hades—stray blossoms somehow growing there, picked in an interval of despair.

There was something cold in Alan's nature that frightened her. He was in love with her, was more idealistic about their union than she could be ; but she knew he did not love her. No warmth of his nature shone on her. He had often great charm, a charm not unlike a child's, selfish and sweet. But she felt the essential narrowness of his nature, its selfishness and weakness. She felt at the same time her own incapacity to deal with life and her own weakness, her own selfishness—her unwillingness to be completely engulfed in the life of this man whom she could not quite like. She hoped that in this sad defeat which she foresaw, she could behave with dignity and kindness ; for she sometimes saw her future, when she allowed herself to think of it at all, as a long retreat from life, harassed by emotional difficulties, always losing ground, with no possible happy outcome. She was fighting in a lost cause. Her only victory would be to remain unembittered and uncomplaining.

Alan, she thought, really disliked woman though he liked women and made his friends

chiefly among them. He had the unpleasant scorn
of a sort of imitation Schopenhauer for the bodies
of women—heavier and clumsier than those of
men, subject (he said) to the ugly deforming pro-
cesses of child-bearing : for their minds which
seemed to him meaner in little things, duller, less
fanciful, and vigorous than men's.

" You haven't got most of the weaknesses of
your sex," he often said to Mariana, but this only
irritated her ; she did not want to be excused as
unwomanly.

He offended some strong, natural thing in her
when he talked about women having children.
" Their minds asleep for nine months and then
screaming in labour like animals." There was an
almost hysterical disgust in his manner of speaking. He felt it as a wrong to humanity that women
should ever become pregnant. Mariana's whole
nature opposed him. She knew that he was wrong.
She could not see how the whole natural order
of life could be disgusting. It was an hysterical
symptom to think so. And his attitude obscurely
wounded her. For under happier circumstances,
she would have been glad to have children, even
many children. She felt that there was something
thin and unnatural in a love-making that was
careful to remain not only physically but mentally
sterile.

She supposed also that in Alan's deepest thought she must be a coarse animal creature only restrained with difficulty by his foresight from performing these disgusting functions and saddling them both with a wretched, unwanted little animal. Her pride as a woman was wounded. Her self-confidence, never strong, suffered a further defeat. For while she did not believe that woman deserved to be scorned, or that Alan was sufficiently a woman's superior to be able to look down on her, she felt herself a member of a race as it were inferior and despised, not through actual inferiority, but as if from some difference in colour or nationality.

But at the same time she felt sorry for Alan, and she thought he was typical of their generation and kind, afraid of responsibility, afraid of reality, building themselves a thin wall of song, pitched in a minor key, against the world with its coarse passions and imperfect beauties.

By the beginning of August Alan had begun to grow tired of the monotonous life at Looe, and they returned to London. As they sat in the train which took them from Liskeard to London, Mariana looked wistfully out at the quiet country places she was leaving. Her short time of peace was at an end. Pictures of Looe appeared in her mind and disappeared. Gulls clustered thickly on

a row-boat in the river, the river at low tide with
the boats lying on their sides on the bare paved
bed, a child's funeral with six fishermen in blue
jerseys carrying the small coffin up the steep
streets to the cemetery on the hill where she had
once gone with Mrs. Pengethorn to put flowers
on Mr. Pengethorn's grave. They were drifting
away, already growing dim. London loomed before them. She was afraid of it.

They decided that they must have a flat. They
were tired of lodgings, and while they looked for
it, they took a temporary room in Chelsea. It was
so awful that they thought it funny, knowing that
they need not stay. There was one gas jet high
up on the wall. This was partly plugged up so
that it gave hardly any light. They slept together
on a narrow iron cot, and Mariana thought that
there must really be some physical affinity between
them, some natural suitability of their bodies, even
if not of their minds, to let them sleep soundly so
close together on so narrow and hard a bed.

She finally found a small furnished flat in
Whiteland's Row and liked it because it reminded
her a little of Patchin Place. The houses were old
and belonged to an estate which took little care
of them and let them to an artist with a Scottish
name who lived in what was literally a ruin in the
back garden. At one time he had lived in a

caravan there, but when he married he felt a need of more room and moved into the ruin.

Mariana took an apartment from the widow of an Anglo-Indian general. The very day that she moved in the Scottish artist came to see her and told her that the general's widow had no right to sublet. " But I'm only too glad to get rid of her," he continued. " I wish she'd always sublet. She's like so many of these Anglo-Indians—thinks people who stayed at home in England and minded their own business are her inferiors and treats us all like natives ; I've had two lawsuits with her already, but I can't get rid of her. She comes of good people too, and the old general was a fine old soldier."

" Was he killed in India ? " Mariana asked.

" Killed at home ! " said the Scotchman with a look of malicious intelligence, and closed the door softly behind him.

They lived on the ground floor, and liked it because they could sit in the back garden when it was sunny. But the sitting-room in front was dark because great elms hung above the large bay window. And when it rained, as it so often did, the rain dripped from the leaves down the panes mournfully.

The man who lived above them had recently returned from a lunatic asylum. His face was blank and kind. He played at simple games with his little daughter in the garden, and spoke to Mariana when they passed each other with amiable courtesy and a perfectly vacant smile. She was glad that he seemed happy, happier and gentler than other people, and hoped that his little daughter would inherit his happiness and not his weakness of mind.

Alan at that time went much to the British Museum Reading Room. He spent entire days there, and was allowed as a regular reader to have lunch in the tea-room, a privilege usually reserved for the staff.

Sometimes he would take Mariana with him and she would wander up and down the dim corridors looking at grey man-headed lions from Assyria and white goddesses from Greece.

They would meet for tea in the tea-room, the door of which is so well concealed behind the second mummy case in the Egyptian room that few people have ever found it. There they served a special kind of bath bun of great excellence which Alan preferred to all others. It was an event when he first took Mariana to tea there. He watched her closely to see if the bath buns were producing their proper effect and was gratified when she declared them the best she had ever tasted. This quality in Alan, like a schoolboy taking her to his favourite tuck-shop, was very endearing. His preoccupation with little, material things was often attractive and diverting. At other times it could be unpleasant. He said one day he had thought of buying her a Roman coin for a keepsake. " But then I thought you were sure to lose it," he added disparagingly.

There was a meanness in this careful foresight that depressed her ; and she answered " Well, if I had, it would have pleased me first." Later he bought one for her, but its charm was spoiled already.

He always harassed Mariana about money. He thought she was extravagant, and she probably was by nature, but now she spent as little as possible. They were both afraid of running short of money in a strange country. Alan took charge of all the money, and gave Mariana what she asked for housekeeping, but she had a perverse pride which made her ask for as little as possible. She would take half-a-crown in the morning and with it buy the cream for next morning's breakfast, and the rolls, the vegetables and meat or fish. If there was anything left, she would spend it on lunch or sometimes save it to pay the admission fee to one of the picture galleries, or buy an eightpenny ticket at a cinema where some dark German film was unrolling its strange story.

She did not have quite enough to eat, for Alan had his largest meal at the Museum and at night they had cold meat and salad. And for lunch, Mariana seldom had anything but bread and milk, or a bun and an apple. She began to get thin again.

One dark day, he came back from the British Museum with something done up in a brown paper bag which he gave her laughingly. On opening it she found a card of pinchbeck jewellery sold for a shilling by a pedlar in the Strand. It was the kind of thing some poor apprentice might buy for his servant sweetheart and Mariana was enchanted. These toys gilded with a gold almost as brief as fairy gold seemed so pretty in idea to her. She wrote a poem for Alan about them.

> *My lover came to me to-day*
> *And brought me pins and golden rings.*
> *He bought them for me in the Strand.*
> *An Irish pedlar sold the things.*
> *I know they are not really gold*
> *But they are glittering golden bright.*
> *I think he loved me well to-day*
> *Though he may tire over night.*
> *But I shall wear my golden pins*
> *And mock the one who doubts their hue.*
> *And I shall kiss his gay young mouth*
> *Who will not kiss it old or true.*

But Alan did not like the poem. He did not want Mariana to say that he would not be true to her or that they would no longer be together when they were old. Mariana wondered how he could think it possible that they would be. And yet when sometimes at night she thought that they might be separated, that she might be forced by her unhappiness to leave him, she could not bear the idea. But when she thought of living always with him like this it frightened her. She remembered an imitation of Chinese poetry, she could not remember who had written it.

When the princess found that she had married a dragon, she sent a gift of daffodils to her lover of former years.

She liked to think of the princess hopeless in the dragon's castle, remembering past springs and sending a pot of daffodils to the one who had loved her in happier years.

Mariana felt that she herself belonged by some innate characteristic to the race of those who are unhappy, lonely, abused. If she had not begun life as a child of poverty and become the slave of a cruel woman, the abused creature of some brutal man, it was through some unaccustomed kindness of fate. Little girls married against their will long ago to indifferent, drunken husbands, nut brown maids deserted for richer, fairer brides, they were all her sisters by nature. There was some fatal passivity in her nature as in theirs that brought their doom upon them from the infinite storehouse of the world.

Mariana knew that her health was failing. She grew thinner, and then she began to have night sweats. She would wake in the night and find her neck wet and the curling ends of her hair as drenched as if she had been swimming in a lake. Consumptives, she had heard, have night sweats, but she thought that perhaps there might be some other cause for them. She did not cough and did not think of taking her temperature. She felt strong, only tired. No doubt she could get through the winter somehow and when the spring came they would go back to the country, and she would get quite well again. She knew fresh air was the main thing if your lungs were weak. But Alan did not like to have the window opened more than a crack in winter. If Mariana insisted, he would let her open it wide, but would complain of the cold. This nightly struggle depressed her so much that she gave it up.

Then there were days when she felt better— days when the weak sun shone and she went walking with Alan in Hyde Park or Kensington Gardens and felt almost well. This tiredness was nothing ; it would pass.

The flat was not a great success, partly because Mariana was not a good housekeeper. She had learned to cook quite well, but she had no talent for order and now, tired and listless, she could not cope with the cleaning. There was dirt and disorder ; Alan was always complaining of it. It interested Mariana to notice that he would complain if something were left on the floor or table that should have been elsewhere, but it never occurred to him as possible that he might move it himself. He was neither neat nor orderly himself, and that added to her difficulties. She realised that Alan had a just complaint in the fact that she could not manage better. But life seemed too much for her.

If Alan began to embrace her after dinner and they fell asleep and did not wake up till it was time to go to bed again, she could not wash the dishes then, she would have kept Alan awake, and yet if the dishes were still unwashed in the morning, it made a further difficulty. She could not imagine how poor wives and mothers managed. She felt great admiration for them.

But things were sometimes happier and better. Christmas came, and they went to almost all the pantomimes in London, and thought *Jack and the Beanstalk* the best.

The winter dragged on. It was a terrible winter

—fog after fog obscured the day. There was one which lasted two days and two nights. It was so dark at mid-day that flares were burning in the Strand in a vain effort to direct traffic, which presently became so dangerous that it almost ceased. Mariana going with Alan to a matinée of *Treasure Island* forgot the time of day and thought that they were going to a night performance. The fog could be tasted. It could almost be felt. It filled their throats, half choking them. Mariana coughed and felt as if her lungs were filled with some alien element. She wondered that it was possible to breathe at all.

As they came out of the Underground at Sloane Square and were walking past the barracks, they suddenly saw, lying in the street, near the pavement the body of a woman. She had been knocked down by a bus which had gone on its way through the fog, the driver never knowing what he had done.

The woman lay perfectly still, her pathetic, ugly hat had been knocked half off, and her grey hair straggled over the collar of her cheap coat. There she lay apparently dead in the foggy light of the street lamps. It all looked quite unreal, and Mariana stood staring down at the huddled figure, hardly believing it was there. Before she could move, a policeman appeared. Some spectator had called him, and a little crowd gathered around the woman, coming from nowhere, silently out of the fog. She knew there was nothing she could do to help and went on with Alan.

But what horrible place was she in where the air choked you when you breathed, and a poor woman lay dying unnoticed in the streets? The monstrous traffic of London horrified her. This was a dreadful place.

If she had been well and happy, she would have come no doubt to love London, for even as it was there were places she grew attached to—the British Museum where she dreamed over colour prints of Blake, or wondered at the gold torques found in ancient British graves, or gazed at the Elgin Marbles, and remembered how the eyes of John Keats had also mirrored these beautiful shapes.

But, unhappy, lonely and more and more ill, she seemed sometimes to be wandering in purgatory. Alan, though he still made passionate love to her, was nervous and depressed himself and scolded her constantly. She felt too hopeless to try to escape. This was her life. She thought that she would die in London on some dark, foggy night, alone.

She was growing really ill. She could see it very well though she never spoke of it to Alan. One day her great amethyst ring, which had belonged to her great-grandmother, slipped from her hand and fell on the floor, and she realised how thin her hands had grown. She held them out and looked at them, wondering how thin they would have to be before her body would become unfit to hold its life any longer. But she still felt strong, she decided, only tired.

It was unfortunate that her one friend, McLeod, was travelling on the Continent, and she felt lonelier than ever. Alan occasionally went to the house of some writer whom he had met, but he did not take Mariana with him for he did not like the habits of domestication which going about with a wife implied. Mariana realised that he was like a perverse Peter Pan who could not bear to grow up, and rather sympathised with him about it, but it added to her distrust of life and of him. She realised that he was not a person with whom it was possible to live a life of dignity or security. It would be impossible to live with him and keep much self-respect.

There was something in her nature that longed to give itself generously to love ; and in that desire she always tried to turn the current of her life into the narrow channels he made for it, but it ran slowly and sadly in them. It was no use, it could not run uphill. She felt that if she stayed with

Alan, she might be made like him, and this she could not bear. And she wondered why she shuddered so at the idea of this metamorphosis, for she did not think of him as a bad man, and she was conscious of weaknesses in herself that troubled her. She had always wanted to be good. She had almost a religious desire to be perfectly loving and kind, to be full of charity as defined by St. Paul—" the charity that suffereth long and is kind and thinketh no evil." She understood why girls in times past, even apart from a wish for chastity or the force of a religious vocation, had retired to cloisters to keep themselves away from men, for she felt that she could not be good or kind as long as she was with Alan. She wore his livery, and she could not be herself.

The winter had turned, spring was approaching slowly, but Mariana felt sometimes that she could not wait. Spring would come too late. Something in her, she did not know whether it was her life or perhaps her capacity for happiness, would not survive to see it.

And then one day she had a letter from Sigrid, who had spent the autumn with an uncle in Sweden and lingered on there into the winter, but now was returning to America. She wrote that she would come out of her way and stop in England to see them.

Mariana was delighted. Sigrid was coming—
her old friend and companion. But Alan was
jealous. He thought again as he had done in New
York that Mariana was too fond of her old friends.
It was excessive. He would not exhibit his feelings
like that ; he had a proper reserve ; he did not
have such excessive feelings. And how could she
show more pleasure in them than in him? He was
more charming. He was her lover. It was he who
had taught her to respond to caresses and to kiss
him back. She was an unsatisfactory wife, she
was a bad housekeeper. And he began to scold
her because she had burned the bottom of a
saucepan. He felt a sense of relief, of restored self-
confidence. This was what was wrong. Mariana
was incapable. That was the trouble.

Alan would not let Mariana have Sigrid to stay
with them. And she had to admit that he was
probably right : there was little spare room. So she
found Sigrid a funny little room over a stationer's
shop on King's Road and hoped she would be
amused by it. It was fusty and dingy but the
blonde, plump comfortable-looking woman who
let it seemed a kind creature and after all Sigrid
would be with them most of the day.

But it was a grief to her that she could not have
a guest. She remembered her grandmother's story
of a visit her father paid to New York. He went

to call on a friend who had a new and up-to-date and handsome apartment, but it had only one bedroom. " And where will he put his guests ? " demanded her father, in horrified accents. A world in which you had no room to put a guest in was unthinkable to him. It was almost as shocking to Mariana.

The day came at last when Sigrid would arrive : they went to meet her at Waterloo. The train stopped and they saw a red head at the window. It was she.

But Sigrid staring back at her friend could hardly believe her eyes. Mariana was so changed. She had grown very thin and her eyes, always large, looked enormous, but still not large enough to fill their hollow sockets. Sigrid was terribly shocked. What have they done to her ? she thought, she looks as if she were dying. She greeted Alan feeling an antagonism that she could hardly hide : this must be his fault.

For Mariana's sake she tried to be gay as they drove back to Chelsea in a taxi. And for the first two days of her visit everything went well. Mariana blossomed out so much in the pleasure of seeing her that Sigrid wondered if her first impression could have been exaggerated. But no, she observed her closely. She was animated, and still lovely in Sigrid's eyes, and at times could still laugh like a child ; but she was extremely thin, and Sigrid believed that she was feverish ; she questioned her about her health, and she made light of it, though she asked Sigrid what she thought her night sweats came from, and Sigrid felt a clutch at her heart. She was sure now what was wrong. But what was to be done about it ? She felt convinced that Mariana's only chance of getting well was to go to some brighter climate, to live outdoors, probably to leave Alan. She did not see how the sick girl could ever improve if she lived with Alan.

She imagined that Mariana suffered from his sensual demands now that she was so frail. She knew that his fault-finding was depressing and irritating ; even in her presence he did not entirely control it. And although she could not quite tell where the real trouble lay, she saw how mistaken was their life together. It was Mariana's inability to cope with practical affairs that was the outward and tangible cause of Alan's chief complaints. But there was something beneath that, for she was not really so bad a housekeeper. If Alan had been tidier or more helpful himself or if he had willingly offered her money to have a charwoman in once or twice a week, she could have managed the house fairly well.

It was the actual scrubbing and cleaning up

173

after two untidy people that she could not manage. Her meals were very good, simple and well balanced.

Sigrid thought that Alan was trying to defeat Mariana in some emotional struggle, and that Mariana could not yield. She thought that she was almost insanely yielding in outward things, she yielded to Alan in everything. She behaved as if his desire of the moment was the current of the universe with which she turned. And she was much too nice about doing little things for him. Why should Mariana get midnight coffee for Alan when she was obviously exhausted by that hour? Why shouldn't he get his coffee himself sometimes? She was no more accustomed to doing it than he. Sigrid thought that her sweetness of manner was not due to love for Alan, but to early training and natural gentleness, and she was astonished that Alan seemed to take entirely for granted everything that Mariana did for him, and to complain that it was not better done. She was a thorough feminist and resented it that service on a woman's part should be so taken for granted. And her love and admiration for her friend made her think it fantastic that Mariana should wait upon Alan at all.

And still she wondered where the deepest struggle between them was taking place and upon what ground. She thought that Mariana would not yield, did not know how to yield, but that she might die of the struggle, if they were not separated.

She decided to sound Alan himself—he never spoke as if he noticed any change in Mariana. So one day she waited till Mariana went out to the kitchen to prepare lunch and said " Alan, don't you think she looks ill ? " She did not want to alarm him.

But he replied calmly, " Oh, I don't think so. She's a bit thin. It's probably the climate. She'll be all right in the summer." So he had noticed nothing ! It was extraordinary to her that Alan could live with Mariana and not see the change in her. She supposed it had happened so gradually that he had got used to her new look. Time was slipping by. She thought she had better try Mariana herself.

At the first opportunity she got Mariana alone. " Mariana, I don't think you are well. I want to take you to a doctor."

" But I am all right, really," protested Mariana. She did not want to go to a doctor. He would confirm her fears, he would fix some disease upon her, and she would really have it.

But Sigrid insisted and finally persuaded her. Then the girls did not know where to go. Sigrid

175

wanted to take Mariana to a specialist, but she could not tell how to find one. In the end they went to the surgeon on the King's Road. He told them Mariana was very run down. "I'm not sure there's not something a little wrong in the right lung," he added. "If she could go to the country, it would be better." He did not seem to think of taking her temperature.

Sigrid let Mariana go out of the surgery ahead of her. "Wait for me a minute," she said and closed the door again. "I'm sure she's really ill," she said to the doctor. "I've been watching her. I'm sure she has fever. Could you tell me the name of a lung specialist?" Her anxiety was too urgent to allow her to be polite ; it broke through ordinary formalities. And the surgeon who was a good man perceived it and sympathised with it. He sat down at his desk again and wrote out an address in West Kensington. "Take her there," he said. " Tell him I sent you if you want to. He's not one of the best known, but he is as good as any of them, I think. And he's a very charming man. You'll like him. He's an Irishman. He'll take a special interest in your friend because she's so young, and beautiful. Even doctors, you know, are sometimes moved by youth and beauty. Here you are. I hope you'll find there's nothing really wrong."

Sigrid stopped at the Chelsea Post Office to telephone for an appointment with the specialist for the unwilling Mariana. The telephone infuriated her. She had never seen an English telephone before. Mariana might die while I try to get this beastly number, she thought as she wasted her sixth penny. But she succeeded at last in making an appointment for the next day.

Mariana, still protesting a little, walked with Sigrid to Kensington. It was a lovely day—the first really spring-like day they had had. There was only a slight haze of smoke in the air.

The specialist looked at Mariana with interest as the surgeon had predicted.

He examined her carefully and was not very satisfied with what he found. " I'd say she's in a pre-tubercular stage," he said to Sigrid. " In fact, I think there's activity going on now, because she has some fever, but I can't actually hear anything. She ought to be got out of London immediately, taken to the country. A high, dry climate is best of course, but I think she'd be all right in Norfolk if she doesn't want to leave England. It seems to me she has some mental trouble. She's nervous. Is she unhappy with her husband ? "

" Yes," said Sigrid. " She'll never get better while she's with him."

" Can't she go back to America and visit her family for a while ? "

" She has no family, but she could go if I could persuade her to. She has a small income of her own."

" Try to persuade her. She evidently can't live here."

Mariana's mind as she left Kensington was actually relieved. The doctor had done no more than tell her what she had always secretly known— in fact it was not so bad as she had thought. Sigrid was amazed to see that she was unfeignedly gay, and felt angry with her for not being more worried. " Mariana," she said abruptly, " you're coming back to America with me."

" Oh, but I can't, Sigrid. I can't leave Alan, and I haven't any money."

" You must, Mariana. Can't you see that you're dying here? Didn't you hear what the doctor said? He said ' She can't live here.' I won't leave you here to die."

Mariana felt a wave of self-pity. It was sad to die so young in this dark place. Yet hopeless as it was a little seed of hope began to grow in her mind. If she could not live here, surely she was justified in going away. This physical weakness might be the key that would unlock the prison in which her mind lay. For the instinct of self-preservation, if it were once roused, would carry her far. She would not stay here and die. She would go away and begin life over again. Her mind seemed to stretch itself as if it were loosed from old chains that had bound and cramped it. And yet she was conscious of a sort of sore misery at the thought of really leaving Alan. She deliberately shut out that part of her consciousness.

And it was in this manner that Mariana left Alan. As she had married him, borne on some fatal tide, the same tide turning seemed to sweep her away from him, still in a dream. He was angry with her and said she had hardened her heart against him. Then he blamed Sigrid, and said it was her fault. Mariana had done very well alone with him. She was not really ill. The summer was coming and they could go to Cornwall again. He was consumed with a jealous pain. His girl was leaving him. She would not stay, nothing he said seemed to reach her. Some power outside either of them was taking her away from him. It was almost as if she were dying, gradually she appeared to become less conscious of him, as if her personality were drawn away even before her body left him.

The excitement of his senses made him constantly embrace her. But her senses seemed dimming, failing in this withdrawal. She responded to him through sweetness and compliance, but he could see she no longer took any pleasure in his caresses. She was hidden from him behind the wall of indifference she had deliberately made between them.

And so she left him, like a person half anæsthetised against pain. She smiled at him sadly, and the train starting separated their hands. He thought that her cold fingers slipped from his like the fingers of a dead girl, or like the fingers of some sea-girl slipping down, down away from him into her own cold element.

Mariana on the boat had a feeling of escape and relief and at the same time was aware of great pain somewhere, which her nerves were too deadened quite to feel. She lay in her berth and listened again to the waves against the cabin side in a sort of careless dream. Sometimes Sigrid came in or went out or read aloud to her. She felt numb and not unhappy.

Alan turned away from the train ; he was glad it was all over. The thing had happened. Mariana was gone. Never again would he feel quite his old boyish self-confidence in his youth, his charm, his power. The thing he had most wanted had changed in his hand, and he had not been able to hold it.

He sat in a park reading the daily paper while

the sun shone, and then he bought himself a ticket for the Coliseum. He did not want to go home quite yet. And his new room would be empty. The changing scenes of the music-hall diverted him, though he was conscious at the back of his mind that there was something the matter.

But as he walked away from the theatre his whole trouble came back upon him, weighed heavy and sad on his mind. Mariana had gone. He could not keep his girl. She had tired of him. She had not left him for another lover, but only because she wanted to be away from him. He had come to depend on her and now she had left him alone. He thought of her slim, white body and a sad lust troubled him. He would not lie in Mariana's arms to-night or any night. Well, there were other girls, and he was conscious that this thought ran dancing through his mind like a young girl itself. He felt a delicate lightening of his spirits.

When Mariana reached New York she hardly knew what to do. None of her friends were there, and Sigrid was going on to Chicago. She could not remain in New York all summer; it would be almost as bad as staying in London. She wrote therefore to ask for her old cottage in the mountains. It would be healthy there and cheap.

She went by train instead of taking the little river-boat. For she had no lover now to caress her while the lapping water lulled their thoughts to sleep. And the river where it ran beside the train looked cold and swift and deep.

A little later she sat at tea by the warm fire in William Hervey's cottage. His white hair and beard gleamed silver in the twilight, his kind voice told her the news, the scandal. As he did so he laughed. Some of the painters and musicians drifted in and greeted her warmly. One asked her to dinner that night, another to breakfast the next day, another to lunch. She felt happy, welcomed, received. The rain had begun to fall outside ; and its melancholy dripping from the dark boughs of the hemlock deepened the sense of secret security the fire and lamplight gave.

There was a scratching at the door and some-one opened it. A great red hound came in. It was Hector. Gravely he made the rounds of the company, but they were all disappointed that he paid no more attention to Mariana than to the rest. She was sad to think that he had forgotten her in so short a time. But when she got up to go, he followed her and he hardly left her again, all summer sleeping beside her bed at night and lying at her feet by day.

But her first night in the woods was very sad.

The friend with whom she had dinner brought her back to her cottage and lit the lamp. But after he had gone, she realised that she had no matches. Once she put out the lamp she would be in the black woods alone with no light until dawn came. Unwillingly, she blew it out and crept into the cold bed. Hector wandered in and out, chasing rabbits and returning again, startling her as he ran through the bushes towards her or when she felt rather than saw his great, dark form in the doorway. He would come up to the bed and lay his head on her hand to make sure she had not departed again while he was gone ; and she would shrink away from him a little, half thinking in the darkness that he was some wolf come to devour her. She lay awake until the first grey light came irradiating her fear.

She was not used to being afraid, but she had slept so long in Alan's arms that she was afraid of this empty universe. Walls of blood and bone had kept away the dark, the cold, the night fear. Ages long, man and woman, like warm beasts had slept together huddled close against the cold. It was that ancient security for which she longed. The night, the dark empty night was around her. It was as if no one else were alive and she was alone in the universe. She wondered how she could ever endure it.

The next day, with the sun shining, she almost forgot her loneliness and fear. She made a round of visits among the studios with Hector following her and lying beside her when she sat down. He lay always from that time onward with his head actually touching her feet, so that it was impossible for her to move without waking him. He was apparently afraid that she might steal away and leave him again.

Mariana was touched by the pleasure these artists showed at her return. But she had a rather melancholy feeling that they never treated her quite as one of themselves, but almost like a creature belonging to some different order of being—rather as people might treat a mermaid, she thought a little sadly ; for it was the warmth of flesh and blood that she wanted.

She had always felt separated from men and women, felt that she could not come near to them. Alan had broken through this separating wall of air, of thought—what was it ? But she had been so unhappy with Alan, so very unhappy. Melancholy scenes of their life together drifted sadly through her mind. Here and there among them appeared a bright picture. She saw the two of them standing by an old bookstall in Charing Cross Road—he turning over the leaves of a battered volume of Cowper's *Task*, she with her attention buried in the twopenny bin among the dusty waifs and strays there, picking up a single volume of Johnson's *Lives of the Poets* with a broken back, and a battered volume of *The Antiquities of Norfolk*.

They were happy then and on the nights when they went together to some music-hall or panto-mime, or sometimes stood even through an entire performance of some play which they particularly wanted to see and could not get seats for.

What am I doing here alone? she thought. I have no life here. There was my life even if I died in it. She watched the people about her wistfully. And when she saw a man who lived happily with his wife or companion, she looked at them with a pitiful admiration as the damned might look at the blest. For they possessed something she had lost, or had never had—they were happy together.

Her nights were profoundly melancholy. It was always raining. And she would lie awake in the darkness, sometimes dropping a hand to touch Hector's sleeping head, or, lighting a candle to drive away the dark, she would read in a book of ballads—

> *All the trees they are so high,*
> *The leaves they are so green,*
> *The day is past and gone, sweetheart,*
> *That you and I have seen.*

ONE WAY OF LOVE

It is cold winter's night,
You and I must bide alone :
Whilst my pretty lad is young,
And is growing.

In the melancholy, sweet, half happy sadness of old time she found a sad comfort. She was not the first who had lain alone. While she lay so solitary here, sad breaths stirred her candle, old airs troubled the wind. Lying alone she did not lie alone.

She found herself sometimes turning her face in the dark to find another face. She seemed to be seeking a kiss—a kiss she had never had. It grew to be a constant half conscious gesture with her to turn her face on the empty pillow and find again that there was no one there. She wrote a poem about these nights. It ended—

I shut my lips against their weeping
But I lie desolate alone
Turning my face for yours unsleeping.

She sent the poem to Alan. It was not a cry to him really. Once she had written down the words, it had become a poem, almost as if someone else had written it. But Alan was profoundly moved by it.

" I did not know you missed me so much," he wrote, " I will come over as soon as I can get a passport."

It was the end of August when he arrived.

The *Leviathan* came slowly, awkwardly into the dock. Mariana, looking up at the clustering, pale faces above her, could not see Alan among so many. Then suddenly, she saw him. He with his quicker eyes had already perceived her and was trying to attract her attention. She saw a tall young man, strong and graceful. His hat was in his hand and his bronze, waving hair shone gold in the afternoon sunlight. His fair, brilliant colouring made him seem more alive than the paler Americans around him. But Mariana knew with a little sinking at the heart that she did not love him. She was not even sure that she was glad he had come.

While they stood talking on the dock waiting to go through the customs she stole sidelong looks at him. She thought, looking at him as at a stranger, that he was attractive, good looking and amusing. Were they really married ? Had she really lived with him ? Would they go to bed together to-night ?

Mariana had cut off her hair since Alan had seen her. She pulled it half behind her ears, and its heavy mass curled on her neck. She took off

her hat to show it to him as they stood on the
dock, and he thought it beautiful. He thought her
more elfish than ever, for all her hair seemed
streaming backward as if blown by some wind
which touched no head but hers. People turned
to look at her, but she was as usual quite unconscious of it and to-day Alan did not care. He had
often resented the fact that people stared at Mariana, and blamed her for it. Once to tease him
she said, " Perhaps it's because they think I am
good looking."

" It isn't," said Alan, " it's because they think
you're queer looking." And Mariana laughed
with pure delight in his honesty.

His honesty was the quality she most liked in
him. If he said a thing, it was what he really believed, or at any rate thought he believed. If she
showed him a poem, he said it was good if he
thought so ; if he thought it bad he said so with
equal frankness. You knew his praise was not flat-
tery, and with him you knew the worst. No ugly
thoughts lay concealed to leap upon you later—
uglier and more dangerous, when the leash of
control could no longer hold them. He would tell
you what he thought—his thoughts were no worse
than his words.

Meanwhile they stood talking quietly. Alan had
brought a gift, a ring of dark green jade, carved

in the shape of two struggling dragons. It was too big for her thin fingers ; she would have to get a guard, but she slipped it on and held her hand shut to keep it from falling off.

At last they were alone in the hotel room Mariana had taken. As soon as the door was closed behind them Alan took her in his arms.

So many nights she had lain desirous of kisses, of embraces, but now she felt nothing. It was an unfortunate time in the lunar cycle of her life and she was recovering from a cold as well. She felt jaded and tired. Her body seemed as if anæsthetised. She tried to respond as if she desired his embraces. But he saw that he had not pleased her, and was disappointed.

" Don't kiss me on the mouth, I have a cold," she said.

" What do I care for that ? " he replied, and groaned with the half sweet pain of lust.

But she felt that they both were disappointed in this meeting. Something was lacking. And when they returned to the mountains and lived in the woods hung with the glory of autumn, something was lacking still.

Though he embraced her often and passionately she knew that he did not desire her as he had once done. And her desire for him, which had always been the reflection in her mind of his desire, paled too. It became abstract again, disconnected itself from him, became a young girl's wish for unknown love.

She thought that he had made love to other girls in London after she had left him, and that this love-making had somehow broken the delicate thread stretched between them as long as they had physically loved only one another. Then they had been man and woman separated from the rest of the universe. He had been man for her : she had been woman for him ; it was no longer so. By leaving him, she had changed everything. Now though he still loved her, she had ceased to be woman, she was a woman ; among many she was the most desired, she was no longer the only one.

In the bright autumn weather she improved wonderfully in health. She seemed really well again and walked with Alan for miles over the country roads, Hector running beside them.

She noticed a new thing in her emotional relations with Alan, that he no longer always tried to please her physically as he had once done. Now he often got a pleasure, she believed, in taking her body when it was unprepared, in having his way regardless of the pain it gave her to be taken so unprepared, or perhaps enjoying it. She could not tell whether he did this because it was simpler, and he had grown weary of the trouble it took to please her, or whether it was a sadistic thing, whether he enjoyed this sudden attack as if he took an ignorant bride or carelessly used a prostitute.

But it did some secret injury to her spirit ; she felt misused, unappreciated—felt a little that he used her instead of a prostitute simply to relieve a physical need, without passion and without love. Then again he would make love to her tenderly, considerately and passionately. Time had helped them to a better mating of their bodies, and Mariana was less agitated than she had been before.

All through the fall of the year they stayed on in the mountains. William Hervey had lent them a more comfortable house, and though the snow drifted under the door and lay upon the floor in piles which the heat inside was not great enough to melt, they lingered on until after Christmas. And it was a sleigh with jingling bells that took them to the station at last.

They found an inexpensive apartment in Patchin Place. Their windows looked down the little, open court. There were two small rooms and only an open fireplace for the winter cold. They bought a wide couch to sleep on, two wicker chairs and a kitchen table with drop leaves, and two bookcases for Alan's thousand books, always the most important part of their furnishing. Mariana brought out of a battered trunk her cashmere shawls and her brocade curtains, the silver candlesticks, and the mirror with the perching eagle, which had returned with her from England.

But the next morning, waking in this strange room, she suddenly began to cry. Alan scolded her bitterly. He said she was never contented, that she had wanted to come to Patchin Place, and now she was dissatisfied ; nothing would suit her.

But it was not that. Waking she had suddenly felt that something had been forgotten, had not been brought to this new dwelling. She was like an Etruscan girl whose household gods had somehow been unpropitiated and had remained behind in the old dwelling, and who wept because there was no Lar of the new hearth. She supposed that what was absent was love.

Mariana learned to love Patchin Place. The small court with its row of ailanthus trees before the little, old, yellow brick houses always delighted her. She loved to lie on the couch under the window and watch the clouds in the sky and the shadow of the pigeons, as the pigeon-scarer on the roof drove them out in long flights. She often lay so while Alan sat writing at the table. She liked to make up the bed on the couch and go to bed there while Alan still wrote or typed. The feeling that someone was awake and working was curiously warm and pleasant. She thought it came from some nursery memory—a grown person was still awake and stirring about. Everything was safe. She would drift off to sleep in a drowsy happiness.

Mariana had felt revived and well when they came down from the mountains, but as the spring came in chilly and sweet, she had begun to feel ill. She felt oddly that it was the world around her that had changed. The air had grown too heavy to breathe, a stronger force of gravity held her limbs. What was it? She had never felt like this before.

It was some weeks before she realised that she might be pregnant. She hardly knew what the signs of pregnancy were—could she really be going to have a child? An extraordinary sadness clouded her mind, for she did not want a child. If things had been different, if she had been a fisherman's wife in a hut on the edge of the sea, if she had been a king's wife in a great palace, her child would have been welcome—but not here, not now. Alan did not want a child, and she had come not to want a child of his.

Perhaps it was not true. She could not be sure by herself. It might be nothing. But why did she feel so ill if it were not true? If this life had begun to grow in her, it must grow changing her body until in agony it tore its way into the air and became another unwanted creature in an ugly world. She thought with a sort of arrogance: the world is not a fit place for my children. It will be better if they are not born.

Days passed, and she became more certain that she was going to have a child. And she felt very ill with that curious impression of disease, as if it were the world around her that was somehow different and wrong.

One night as she sat on the box by the fire, her favourite seat, leaning her head against the chimney corner, Alan was so struck by her melancholy look that he began to scold her for it. He said she was never satisfied, always morbid and unhappy. She looked at him so wearily, with such unspoken sadness in her eyes that he was struck by it and stopped in the midst of his complaint.

" Mariana, is there anything really wrong ? " he said.

" Yes," she said quietly, " I think I am going to have a child."

He stared at her without speaking. She could see that the idea had profoundly shocked and startled him. But when at last he did speak he said quite gently, " Do you want to have a child?"

" No," she said sadly.

There was a cold, wintry wind blowing about the house. They sat silently, listening to its crying.

But the next day he was angry with her ; felt that it was her fault if she had become pregnant. He was careful, she noticed, not to suggest in any way that it was a disgusting state, but she knew very well that he thought it was. She had heard him say too often how shocking he thought it. But perhaps after all she was not going to have a child. Could a doctor tell her ? she asked Alan. He thought one could tell, he was not sure.

She scarcely knew what to do. They were poor. Perhaps the best thing was to go to a hospital clinic. The doctors at the lying-in hospitals would know more about pregnancy than ordinary doctors. She must end this tension of suspense. The same morning she went to one of the maternity hospitals which she had heard was a good one.

She passed through swinging doors into a dark hall. The cement walls of the basement where the clinic was held, seemed to her wet with a perpetual sweat, an unhealthy emanation. A stupid woman took her name. " Do you mean to have your baby here ? " she said.

" But I don't know if I am going to have a baby," said Mariana. " I want to find out." She was given a piece of cardboard with a number on it and told to wait with a long line of women in one of the wet corridors. She found an empty place on a bench and sat down among the others. All around her were women in every state of pregnancy, some in whom no change was apparent, others with only a slight haggardness, many great with child ; several with distended sides seemed to pant as they breathed with animal distress. An hour went by while the women went in to the doctors, one after another. Mariana looked about her. There were Italians and negroes, and Jewish women from the East Side, and Germans and Scandinavians, and she supposed even Old Americans like herself ; but she hardly saw the differences between them. In this place and this hour they all looked to her the same. They seemed to her like animals, like sheep, over-driven, waiting patiently, hopelessly, to be sheared, to be butchered. Suddenly she leaped to her feet. This was a trap—she must get out. She rushed down the corridor and through the doors into the open air.

But she must find out if it were true. She went to the Cornell Clinic. She thought it might not be so bad there.

A young doctor examined her and told her immediately, " Yes, you're certainly pregnant—two months or more."

Mariana started a little as if he had hurt her.

" You'll be all right," he said reassuringly.
" There's nothing to do at this stage except take
care of your health in a general way."

" But I feel so ill," she said tiredly, " so very
ill."

" What is it ? What do you feel ? "

" So tired, and somehow dazed and my heart
runs so fast, it tires me and keeps me awake."

He felt her pulse and took her temperature and
looked searchingly in her face.

" Any history of tuberculosis ? " he asked.

" Yes," she said doubtfully and explained that
she had not been well in London.

" I think you'd better go over to the medical
side and let them look at your lungs ; then come
back to me." He smiled at her. She saw that he
was trying to reassure her, and felt afraid.

On the medical side, they took her temperature,
which was too high, and her pulse, which was too
fast, and left her alone to take off her dress in a
little room.

Presently a young doctor came in. He was very
big and fair and strong, and he seemed for some
reason embarrassed and unhappy. She was tired
and nervous, but the two young creatures tried
pathetically to put each other at ease. He examined
her chest, and asked her a few questions in a low

197

voice and took notes. Then the door opened and an older man entered. She realised that the first man was one of the graduate students for whom the clinic was partly conducted, and had been allowed for practice to examine her first. He retired into a corner and sat silent while the older man examined her again and commented on his findings. She looked at him and noticed the expression of his handsome, young face. It was anxious and sad.

The older doctor seemed troubled and presently called in a colleague, a tall woman with white hair. To her he said, " I think this pregnancy ought to be stopped. I can't find anything in the lungs, but she's got a high temperature and a fast pulse and seems ill. I wish we had an X-ray. Will you examine her and see if you agree with me ? "

She did, and finally stood looking down at Mariana. " Yes," she said.

" You're a writer," the older man said to Mariana, " and you live in Patchin Place. I know it well. You haven't much money, and you don't get much sunlight. You might take a chance on this, if you were going to get the best possible care, but you can't."

" She couldn't, anyway," said the woman. " It's too great a risk, she couldn't stand the strain. She'd lose her child or die before it was born. She mustn't try it. These cases have a bad history."

A bad history, Mariana's mind repeated. She saw a bare hill where a cold wind was blowing. It's very lonely there, she thought.

" What are we going to do about this child ? " the woman was saying almost angrily. " She mustn't get in this state again immediately, she couldn't stand this often."

" She'll be careful and see that it doesn't happen again," said the older doctor gently. " You will probably be able to have a child safely in two or three years," he continued turning to Mariana, " though there will always be a certain danger in it. But if you are anxious to have children, you could try if you take care of yourself."

Mariana sat on the edge of the table still in her white, silk slip. She saw the two doctors standing, looking down at her with a pitying interest. She was tired from the examination and found it hard to breathe, but she smiled up at them. Then she looked at the young doctor, and he gazed back at her as if the sight of her hurt him—and perhaps it did.

She found it hard to get home through the busy East Side traffic. She felt dazed and ill. The noise of the streets seemed like a whirlpool round her head. Yet she stopped to buy fish for dinner at the

Jefferson Market, and finally climbed the narrow crazy steps up to the little flat.

Alan was at home having tea; lying on the couch she told him quietly what the doctors had said. She was perfectly calm—but he caught in her voice a breaking note because she was so tired that talking was difficult.

He was angry and said brutally, "What are you complaining about? You didn't want to have a child. This should suit you perfectly."

She was amazed and realised that though he did not want a child and was angry with her for becoming pregnant, he was angry with her also for not wanting his child.

They seemed to be quarrelling. Mariana had a horror of such scenes. She felt that she was in a sordid situation, and she did not know how to escape from it. Somehow by some unknown road she had come to this particular small high room to sit quarrelling with this young man. She had never meant to come here. It was all a mistake. She had found her way to the wrong house, to the wrong man. But where was the room where she should be, and how could she find it? She had come too far.

Alan left angrily. She felt no longer tired, but very strange. Nor was she sad. She only wanted to escape. Her rising fever and her passionately hurrying heart gave her a restless energy. Where could she go? Could she go to an hotel? She looked in her purse, but found that she had less than a dollar. She was to enter a hospital on Monday. If she could only spend these two days alone, away from Alan! If she could only escape entirely out of this life! Her excitement was failing. She heard the small, sad wind complaining at the window. She was alone, she said to herself, there was nowhere in the world where she could go.

She had been sitting on the couch to talk to Alan—now with a loss of hope and life she laid her head against the wall. Her heart beat so painfully that she could hardly breathe. She looked up at the bare, white-washed walls. Something strange was happening; they were bending towards her. She looked at them incuriously, thinking something must be happening to the world. She stared up at the ceiling—it seemed to be buckling and swaying down upon the walls. And now something was swaying in her brain. The walls rushed together, the room grew darker and darker till everything was blotted out.

She lay on the bed curled in a heap. Dimly she heard a clock striking twelve and idly counted the strokes. She felt rested, refreshed, everything that went before forgotten. She looked at the small, lamp-lit room, at the watermarks on the ceiling with a dreamy pleasure. It was real, and she liked the way that one watermark took the shape of a map of England ; only Ireland was wrong. She liked the shadows on the floor and blackened mantelpiece, merely because they were like that. She felt dreamily content. But she heard steps on the stair : it was Alan. He came in, still angry, and scolded her for not being in bed ; for in this little place it was difficult for them to undress at the same time. She said nothing, but quietly got ready in the tiny bedroom and came to lie beside him.

They lay as far apart as possible—in silence. In a few moments, she heard his sleeping breath, quiet as a child's. But she lay awake for long hours sadly wondering how she came to be here.

The next morning Alan was in a better mood. It was plain even to his rather careless eyes that she was ill, and plain to all his senses that she was beautiful. Her pregnancy and the condition of her lungs had given her complexion an extraordinary transparency : it was flawless, and it seemed to Alan in the early morning light almost translucent as if the sky behind her shone through her face. He turned and took her in his arms and embraced her freely. There was nothing to fear to-day. He need not be careful, need not worry—he could not get her with child now, she was already with child.

When he had finished he went back to sleep and Mariana enclosed in his arm drifted into a troubled, uneasy dream. It was late when they awoke and Alan said that she had better stay in bed ; he would get them a breakfast-lunch. He pulled the tea-table to the bed and cooked eggs and made toast and coffee. They breakfasted pleasantly, talking of books as they had done so often before. It seemed strange to Mariana that she could stop in this drifting current of misery to talk of Hogg's *Life of Shelley*, and for the moment think of nothing else. Outwardly this breakfast might be one of happy lovers, and she suddenly remembered that it was their wedding day.

Later in the afternoon Jack Hasty came in. He was one of the few acquaintances whom Alan was generally glad to see. They told him that this was the second anniversary of their wedding and he said that they must celebrate it and as they could not come out to dinner with him, because Mariana was in bed, he would have dinner sent in from the *rotisserie* and they would eat it beside her bed. He was about to go off to bring in great supplies when Mariana said that she felt better and would get up.

They decided to go to the Bear, a Russian

restaurant on the East Side, which Mariana liked. But Alan after starting out with them changed his mind and said he would not go, he did not feel in the mood for going out to dinner, he would rather read. They realized that some sullen mood had come over him and did not urge him, but went off together.

The Bear was full of Russians talking and laughing to one another, and it was lit with great paper lanterns. Mariana and Hasty climbed up to a balcony and sat eating borsch and black bread and looking down at the busy tables. The balalaika orchestra in crimson and yellow blouses began to play ' The Russian Moon,' and the moonlight of which they played was light and dancing like quicksilver ; then they broke suddenly into the melancholy air of one of the Volga river songs, " Er ch'ab Volga matushka, Er ch'ab ras lubili——"

Mariana knew the words, Ligeia had taught them to her, and her mind went on saying them after the music had ceased and the noisy applause had begun—' If we could be loved for ever.'

She tried to wake herself out of this heavy dream in which her illness imprisoned her to talk to Hasty. She looked at the paper lanterns, and began to speak almost at random.

" These lanterns are, almost of all things I have

seen," she said, " the most perfect symbol of man's pathetic evening gaiety. They glow like artificial man-created moons, they tear if you touch them, and catch on fire and char and are spoiled ; they shine with all our longing for gaiety, for romance which is unattainable. We have cried for the moon and they have given us a paper lantern."

Hasty caught her half articulate feeling. " Yes," he said, " other things from the same evanescent country are toy balloons—so light on the air and so brightly coloured. They escape and go rising out of sight, or they break. Many a child must have had its first inkling of the nature of the world when a toy balloon burst in its face."

" Bubbles are different," Mariana went on speaking from some almost unconscious depth whose images floated up to the surface because her physical weakness thinned the barriers between the regions of her mind, between the dreamer and the waker.

" Do you remember how a bubble appears just before it breaks, how the colours grow deeper and brighter, and gradually begin to swim around and around its surface, faster and faster, until suddenly it breaks and they are gone, and there is nothing but a spray of tiny drops in your face and a little water in your hand ? But it never was sad. The turning colour was a consummation, and it was complete when the bubble broke : then you blew a new one, and it began all over again.

"What extraordinary happiness bubbles gave you when they rose up over the wall and disappeared into the sky ! but almost more—I don't know why—when they fell if you were blowing them from some high place, from a balcony, or out of a window. They fell towards the ground so lightly, so slowly, in a kind of miracle, as if they would go on falling for ever, descending, world after world."

How ill she must be ! Hasty thought, staring at her. Her large too brilliant eyes looked down and mirrored the glowing lanterns, the orchestra swaying to the rhythm of its own music, the moving crowd, and reflected them back unseeingly ; the windows into her mind were too clouded with dim impressions of the past to let them in.

She is almost delirious with fever—Hasty thought—I must take her home—and he called the waiter, and they went out, pushing their way with difficulty between the tables, Mariana following him in a dazed dream which the noise about them swirled around, troubled and confused, but could not break.

* * *

The next day she went to the hospital. Alan went with her in the Elevated, carrying her bag. And together they entered the dark hospital hall.

She felt almost indifferent now. Life was going in this particular way. It hardly seemed to matter. They sat drearily in the waiting-room until a nurse came and took her name and the name of her nearest friend, and gave her a receipt for twenty-five dollars—one week's payment for a bed in a ward. Then an attendant took her bag and began to lead her away to an elevator.

" Good-bye," she said to Alan, smiling and formally giving him her hand ; but he bent and kissed her. There was such a lack of warmth in his kiss that it depressed her.

She lay in a bed in the ward for a long melancholy week while all the associate doctors of the hospital who specialised in tuberculosis or gynecology, examined her and discussed her case. They seemed unable to decide what to do.

She lay, glad to lie still and rest at last, and looked at the white ceilings and the white beds around her. She tried not to be too aware of this cold melancholy place where everyone was ill and in pain.

The woman next her was a kind Jewish mother of five from the East Side. The doctors were trying to mend her body, damaged by too indiscriminate child-bearing.

" I should have come here sooner," she said to Mariana, " then I wouldn't of miscarried my last two times."

Mariana liked her and admired her kind fecundity which grieved not to have a sixth and seventh child. Her husband was a prosperous, small tailor, and they meant to do well by their family. With Jewish generosity she pressed oranges and halvah on Mariana, whose delicate features and dark curled hair seemed to her aristocratically Jewish.

Beyond the Jewish mother was a girl who was there for treatment after a criminal abortion which had left her in a bad condition. She was able to walk about, and Mariana tried to talk to her and lent her magazines because she felt sorry for her. But she could not like her. She seemed a super-ficially sophisticated city product, whose greatest joy would be an evening at a cheap night club with some small business man or travelling salesman, and who lay in bed reading *College Humour* or the last best selling novel with a sulky expression on her rather aggressive, good-looking young face.

Mariana pitied the trouble that had led the girl to some shady surgeon or unpleasant midwife and the pain that she had suffered. But she could not like her. There was nothing likeable about her. She seemed to feel a sort of social shame at her position although the other women did not make any difference in their treatment of her, and the doctors and nurses in such a place were too used to every type of case and too occupied to show surprise at anything. But Mariana felt that the shame which she thought the girl sometimes seemed to exhibit by her sullen demeanour was of the nature of some form of little snobbery, such as not having the proper gloves, or wearing a high neck, when other girls had on evening dresses.

Most of the women in the ward were as rough as truck-drivers, coarse, loud-mouthed creatures, whose silly and obscene talk kept her awake at night until the night nurse with difficulty hushed the ward. She wondered why there is something so repulsive in the coarseness of women, why such women seem so much more unpleasant than similar men. She thought that perhaps the very difference of their reproductive organs had something to do with it. Man's were outside himself, used as a tool, not quite a part of him, but something accompanying him. Women at their worst seemed merely to surround a womb as if they were the sodden clay about a stagnant pool.

The two chief nurses of the ward were a perpetual irritation to her—loud-voiced, hard-faced, roughly efficient women with vulgar manners and coarse jokes. And it irritated and depressed her to be constantly in public, on view, when she felt ill and unhappy.

Alan came to see her in the brief visiting hours. One day he brought her lilacs, cold and wet as if with spring rains. She put a spray beside her on the pillow when she went to sleep. Its scent haunted her dreams with a thin, wistful fragrance.

But Alan's indifference to her trouble saddened her. She did not love him truly, so why should he love her? Why should he not be indifferent? What is one creature's pain to another, unless by birth or lust or habit the hurt flesh is identified with its own?

And yet she felt betrayed. She felt there had been no one to walk with her the short way allowed before the soul, with its *geas* upon it, takes the last lonely step and is beyond cry or comfort. She remembered a sentence from Llewelyn Powys' *Skin for Skin*. " It is only very rarely that even the most clear sighted of us grasp the actual terms of our existence, each tremulous, intellectual soul being set shockingly apart to endure as best it may its own destruction."

At the end of a long, dreary week, she was told they would operate on the following morning.

She felt glad that it was to happen at last and

that she might escape from the hospital in another
week if all went well. She could not regret the
child. Essentially, she had never believed in it ;
as soon as she was sure she was to have a child,
she had been told that she could not have it. It
had never existed in her mind. About the operation she felt only indifference. Alan had showed
distress at the idea that they might hurt her, but
she supposed they would give her some anæsthetic. She seemed to be caught in a trap where
it was death to stay inside. But there was a way
out—narrow and sharp. "Per porte penible à port
plaisant." Was that the inscription she had read
on a wall in the Tower of London? But she did
not think she would awake in some harbour of
heaven. She thought she would wake in grey pain
and return to a life which had ceased to be very
dear to her.

She went to the operating-room with a feeling
of almost abstract interest. They had given her
morphine which seemed rather to exhilarate her.
She even found her dazed state diverting, and was
amused when she discovered that she could no
longer sit up.

In the small room next to the operating theatre,
she smiled so gaily and talked so cheerfully to the
nurses and the young anæsthetist, that they
looked at her in surprise. They were used to the

timidly nervous and the stoically calm, but this strange young woman, they realised, was honestly indifferent. She was anxious not to give trouble and to make the occasion a pleasant one for them, nothing more.

One of the nurses was a young German girl with a singularly beautiful face, calm, lovely and good under waves of shining corn-coloured hair. Mariana heard her pretty, broken accent with pleasure and thought that if that calm face were her last sight of earth she would leave a planet that need not altogether be ashamed of its present inhabitants. But the girl went back into the operating theatre, and the anæsthetist covered her face with a cone of translucent yellow.

" What is it ? " Mariana asked. " Is it ether ? " She was very interested. She had never taken an anæsthetic or seen one given.

They told her it was one of the new gas anæsthetics, but she could not catch the name.

" Will it give me dreams ? " she asked. " I remember the ether dreams William James describes in *Varieties of Religious Experience*. I should so like to dream like that."

" You may," said the young doctor, " but I don't think most people dream at all."

" Breathe deeply now," he continued, and she took quiet deep breaths.

She seemed to be in an open place—the air was clear and light and golden. Then the air grew lighter—golden, golden air. She was on a high place, but the air was growing too light. She breathed too rapidly. She could not catch the air. Her heart ran faster and faster. She was caught in speed. Her blood was racing through her veins. Her heart ran so rapidly that she could not feel it. Every atom in her body seemed to whirl faster and faster. She was being forced out of life. She could not hold it any longer. Faster and faster she was being driven out of consciousness. She tried to stop, tried to hold back.

Her last thought was, "This is annihilation, and I don't think I like it."

Lights—lights—faces that grew larger and drifted away. And rending pain. She thought to herself with a sort of curiosity—I wonder if I can stand this pain ? I don't think I could stand it very long. The faces drifted away, were lost—the pain was gone.

She had wandered too close to the border of the strange dream-land of anæsthesia—a merciful wave of the lethean vapour bore her back into black unconscious peace.

She woke again when they were taking her from the operating theatre to a special ward. A man was smiling down at her and asking her how she was. She tried to smile back at him, but she did not think she had succeeded ; she could not feel the movement of smiling in her face. Her eyes closed again in drugged sleep.

She woke fully in a small ward. It was a cold, sunny morning and the windows were open and someone was sweeping the floor. She shivered with cold. She saw a clock on the wall straight in front of her and was amazed to see that the hands stood at 8.30. She had been operated on at 8 o'clock. It was all over and she was wide awake. There was no pain now. Her body felt completely paralysed—she could not feel it at all. The cold, dusty air blew through the open windows. She shivered and the attendants, who had been moving about the ward in which she awakened with an indifference that made her feel as if she were invisible, suddenly seemed to become aware of her, closed the window and brought more blankets.

The nurse had a southern voice and Mariana began to talk to her about the South. She felt curiously light and exhilarated, almost gay. For hours she could not feel her body at all. Then a dull pain began—a bruised, horrid hurting. She did not complain, but after she had been taken back to the former ward, the nurse told her that the house doctor had left orders to give her morphine that night if she wanted it, and she was glad to have it. She slept a heavy, troubled sleep, waking sometimes with her hair wet and clinging to her neck.

Alan came to see her the next day. He brought with him her Russian friend, Ligeia. Mariana had told no one that she was ill. She had no family, and was somehow unwilling to tell her friends ; but Ligeia had become anxious about her and insisted that Alan should tell her where Mariana was. She came with her arms full of flowers. Mariana was relieved that Ligeia had come and that she would not be alone with Alan. And the presence of the Russian to whom she was very attached and whose rich, melancholy nature suited hers, made her feel suddenly happy and almost gay.

Alan was moved by the sight of Mariana lying in bed almost as white as her hospital gown, made like a monk's robe of coarse white cloth and knotted together at the back of the neck. He sat by her bed holding her hand. He even kissed her before the nurses. " Poor elf," he said sadly as he bent down.

The operation had been performed by the head of the hospital, one of the most famous surgeons in his field, and Mariana was never to have any trouble from it afterwards, but it had been a difficult one and not entirely satisfactory at the time.

Two days later, while she was talking to Alan and Jack Hasty who had also come to see her, she was conscious that the heavy ache in her body was turning to a sharp rending pain and extraordinary, cramping pains began to run down the nerves of her thighs, so that she found it almost impossible to stay still and talk quietly to the two young men.

All night she was in such pain that she grew faint and cold at times, but her young body managed to take care of itself. In the morning, the sharp pain was over, and the measures the doctors discussed proved unnecessary. She recovered rapidly. A week after the operation, Alan took her home.

She had only sat up for an hour or two in the hospital and was very weak. Alan, unused to illness, did not realise it, and had asked some people to tea, thinking to divert her. She went straight to bed, feeling quite helpless when she tried to stand or even sit up straight.

Alan cooked her an egg for lunch and they talked and read until her friends came.

These were Lucio Ferrano, the puppet master, and his wife, Frances Taylor. These two charming, small creatures always seemed to Mariana like

the most skilful of their puppets come to life—
like characters from the puppet opera of De Falla,
in which a little puppet show is given by the great
stringed marionettes : Don Pedro gives his play
from Orlando Furioso until Don Quixote, angry
that right is not triumphing, breaks through the
play and cuts off the heads of the actors. Now the
two sat about her bed like characters come to life,
their expressive actors' faces kind and a little
anxious.

Mariana thought : "Ferrano is like a mediæval
jongleur or rather like a perfect puppet taking the
part of a mediæval jongleur. Human beings never
give you that feeling of intense bright life that he
does. It is only puppets that do or toys in the eyes
of children." He smiled at her, his sensitive face
changing like water swept by wind.

Frances Taylor talked and her gay, wistful
face was white and expressive under its tiny
black skull-cap like the face of a pierrot.

Mariana found herself too weak to get up the
next day and for some days afterwards. Alan was
surprised, he had expected her to be well. He had
never thought she was really ill. But he was re-
markably patient, cooked meals and ate them
with her on the tea-table drawn up to the bed.
He was working late at night collaborating
with a woman who had had some interesting

experiences in Siam, but was incapable of writing them, and he often stayed out very late.

Mariana could see that he was taken with this woman who was much older than he. And she was amused. She thought it was possible that they were having an affair, but it did not seem a matter of any great importance.

" What is she like ? " she asked one day.

" Like a humming bird," Alan replied rather sentimentally.

Mariana had a sudden vision of the humming birds she had watched so often at home, busy, fussy, insect-like little creatures sticking their long beaks greedily into the honeyed centre of the flowers they buzzed about, and she could not help laughing. Alan was hurt, and she felt ashamed. She thought it was quite as wrong to laugh at him as to laugh at some child who confidently shows a treasured green camel from a Noah's ark.

He sometimes stayed out until two or three at night but Davenant almost always looked in during the evening, often rather late after a lecture. He would read to her for an hour or so—French poetry often, sometimes German poetry, but this he had to translate to Mariana who knew no German. Once he read Lucretius' wonderful dedication to Venus. Another evening he brought her a book of the Latin prayers used at his public school in England and read them to her. She found she could understand them easily, and lying in bed watching his fine, grave head in the warm firelight, and seeing behind him Alan's writing-table with its bundle of quill pens, hearing the timeless wind blowing outside she almost thought she must be some girl of long ago by whose sick-bed a monk was reading.

When he had gone she would put out the light and lie down to sleep. The wind blew gustily up the crazy stairs, the door into the street stood open. But Mariana with her door unlocked turned to sleep with a strange confidence. She sometimes would not even wake when Alan came in, in spite of the noise and the light.

One morning when she woke she found him lying on top of the bed-clothes with his overcoat spread over him. She had been so quietly asleep that he had been unwilling to stir the covering about her. He woke in the morning, cold but gay, proud that he had managed not to wake her.

Even at this time he was often gay and charming. Davenant coming up the steps one Sunday morning heard them laughing together, entering he saw Mariana lying in bed wrapped against the cold in her scarlet quilted silk dressing-gown. And he never forgot the scene : it stayed in his mind like a brightly lit picture—the small, shabby room with its inadequate fire, the walls covered with books and Mariana's few pieces of china arranged also in bookcases, the grey cold north light of a dark morning falling across the bed where she lay laughing in her scarlet robe and the chair by the fire where Alan sat pouring out a last cup of coffee. The bed was covered with sheets of Sunday papers, and they were reading them, sometimes stopping to read aloud some odd story. It reminded him of a scene from a play; he almost wondered what the play was and what the characters were going to say and do, before his mind was caught back by their gay greeting.

Mariana believed now that Alan had never loved her and was aware of some fatal lack in their life together. His indifference when she was ill had given her a deep distrust of life with him.

When he was most in love with her and most excited by her physical presence she had moved a shallow spring of tenderness in him never stirred before ; now the waters were still and cold again.

She was even half afraid of him, afraid at least of living with him. Her old sense of something wrong came back stronger than ever. She felt, she thought, like someone in a folk tale who marries a man in the likeness of a young lord, but as they ride together on their progress to his home, the trees take on a curious shape. There is something odd, something ominous about the shape of the fields. And the girl does not know whether to stay, or to run into the fearful landscape where a root might clutch her ankle or the trees bring their branches together to bar her road as she sees the face of her husband turning to the face of a dragon man with pointed ears, and knows that she is in his power.

Her sense of fear and distrust seemed to her all the more horrible because on the surface Alan was kinder than usual. And yet she felt sure that if she had had a child, he would have left her or made her life so difficult that she would have been obliged to leave him, knew that there was something sterile and ugly in life undertaken on such terms, was repulsed by this barren ideal which saw something nasty in the simplest, most essential things.

Mariana, lying alone in bed at midnight when Davenant had gone, listened to the cold wind blowing the dirt about the dusty streets, rustling the branches of the ailanthus trees in the court and stirring their young leaves.

She must leave Alan, she thought, must separate herself from him. Something fearful would happen if she went with him further and further into this ominous country where everything was beginning to take an unnatural shape. She was getting stronger. Davenant had taken her that afternoon to sit in the park and she found that the busy streets no longer dazed her. She could have gone alone without fear. Why should she not go ? She could go to Edgewood, get some little house, not in the colony where she had stayed before, but farther off in the woods, where she could be more secluded.

She would retrace her steps from the crooked wood. Evil things might assail her on her way back, but it was better than going on and on until she became herself one of the twisted creatures that would inhabit so crooked a wood. Yet she would be lonely, physically and emotionally so lonely—and she was afraid of loneliness now. She had grown so used to sleeping with Alan, to feeling when she waked an arm about her protecting her from the night. She thought strangely enough that the lack of love-making, of caresses, would trouble her far less than the loss of this. Some sensitive pride in her very body had been wounded of late by Alan's careless embraces, so that even when he was most ardent and most successful in his love-making, she was no longer really under his charm.

For some time after she returned from the hospital he had not embraced her, afraid that he might hurt her. And when he had begun again, his almost exaggerated precautions against making her pregnant had rather discouraged them both.

She did not think it was his caresses she should miss so much as his presence. She felt there was a secret life that could only be lived in company. Alone it would be frightening, like straying too far away from an empty house. When she lay in bed in the warm pool of lamp-light, while Alan wrote late at his table, she was securely, secretly alone as she had never been when she lived by herself. She was more happily alone in her thoughts because there was someone there outside. When there had been no one, she had always been returning to more commonplace thoughts, afraid of going astray in the unexplored regions of the mind.

Now she would be truly solitary. In this fairy-tale wood in which she found herself where any-thing might happen, she would be entirely by herself. She would no longer be protected, even by the white unicorn of virginity—that proud and wild creature—she would be more defenceless than ever. Yet she must go.

At first Alan could not believe that she was serious when she said that she meant to leave him. He realised that this was very different from the former occasion when she had left him in

London. Then it had been partly at least on account of her health. She had only said that she wanted to leave London, not that she wanted to leave him. But now quietly, with no agitation, she said, " I want to go up to Edgewood. I think I could get well there, and I don't want to come back here in the fall. I want to take a place of my own. I think it would be better if we did not live together."

Alan felt baffled by her quietness. She was not leaving him in anger. She was not leaving him for another lover. She had no duty calling her away. She only wanted to go, wanted to leave him, to escape him. Again she was dealing a deep, almost a mortal blow to his pride as a man. He knew that he was skilled in the art of love—strong, young, handsome. But this girl, the only girl he had ever married, the one he had most loved, while he was still kind to her, warm and flushed from his embraces, sat on the edge of the couch they shared and looked at him with dark eyes whose expression he could not read, and told him she wanted to go—she must go, she must leave him. She said it as quietly as she might have said, " I must go to the corner for lettuce," without anger and without grief.

He was baffled. He could not understand her at all. She would end by coming back, he thought.

And if she did not, there were other girls, the world had always been full of girls. They came with every spring, like apple blossoms. Let her go. He felt brutal anger for a moment, wished to punish her ; then his emotion faded in discouragement.

" Have you thought how you are going to live ? " he said. " What you are going to do? You are used to being loved now, to being embraced. Have you thought that you will miss it, need it ? "

" I shall not live the life of a nun," said Mariana sadly.

" You couldn't possibly live a Greenwich Village free-love sort of life, you would die of it. Even apart from the soiling and spoiling of your too sensitive nature, think of the risk of physical contagion in such a life. Half, far more than half the men you meet either have or have had gonorrhœa, probably one in seven has syphilis. Such diseases aren't confined to the lower classes, you know. Anyone is apt to get them. If you became infected, you would never survive it, it would be so horrible to you."

" But I'm not going to begin a life of violent free love," replied Mariana. " I only said I thought that at my age it was unlikely that I would never be made love to again. The very fact that

I've been married would make it more difficult for me to keep men away. They know I am not a virgin. They will not be so afraid of injuring me, or of involving themselves. I can see that my life with people will be more difficult. But if I do have a love affair, it will be with a person who has decent ideas about it. Why should you think that any men who became interested in me must be brutal or shallow or diseased? Why shouldn't I meet someone with whom I could be happy?"

Happy—I never will be happy with anyone, she thought. Something is wrong. In all our crazy, twisted, besotted heads there's nothing with which to make people happy. I am as bad as the rest. I am only different in knowing it. They are complacently self-satisfied in the thought that they can make anyone happy—they are sure that they are good, that they are successful. How stupid we are and how insensitive! And how can we help being so? Each one of us a small bit of animated consciousness enclosed in a bone case, separated by air and space from its fellows with no way of knowing what goes on in any other mind. (It's probably much what goes on in one's own—but it is impossible to be certain.) Queer sounds are all we have to deal with, hot breaths of air of symbolic length shaped by a bit of pointed flesh and clutching teeth to particular syllables. These are all we have to tell us what a man thinks. Is it any wonder we do not know each other? Words, words, words—I try to express the figures I see in my mind with these queer sounds. Another does the same. What he means I have no idea of. His words are jerked from him by explosions of emotion ; so are mine. They are scarcely intellectual in any pure sense at all. Heavens, what is it all about? If I could only once really *touch* another mind, really join thought with thought ! Perhaps we do in physical embraces, but in a moment we are back each in our bony cell, watchful, distrustful, with no means of communication. It is a dreadful situation.

But Alan was still talking. He was working himself into a rage. He was saying that as long as she bore his name, he expected her not to disgrace it. She felt baffled by his conventional arrogance.

" I don't want to bear your name," she said with angry scorn. " I much prefer my own. Anyway, if you haven't stained your name by visiting prostitutes when you were a boy and having numerous affairs with all sorts of women since, I should hardly think that any affair of mine could sully its connotations of purity."

Alan looked at her with angry, injured eyes. She saw that he was in one of the moods when he was unable to stop talking, but would go on and on elaborating a sense of injury. The prospect irritated and bored her.

" I must go out," she said hastily, " I am going to tea with Ligeia."

Alan went on scolding. He could not stop talking at such times. He went on and on for hours. His scolding droned through her mind till it became like the drone of a melancholy black bee gathering a bitter honey from withered flowers. She went out and closed the door. For a moment she had escaped. She would go back late at night and then perhaps his mood would have worn itself out.

She turned down the steps afraid that he might catch her even now. She remembered how in penitent, gentle moods he had called himself the Ogre and called her the Brown Elf. For the moment he was truly an ogre to her. If she stayed, he would destroy her. He would scold away her youth. He would scold her into a dry hag scolding back at him. She was changing already, she felt herself changing. She must leave him.

A few days later, she began to pack her things. Alan's anger had worn out and he was almost willing to let her go. She had hurt him. Perhaps, he thought to himself, it was best.

He saw her off when she took the train to Kingston, kissed her good-bye and said he would come up to see her.

She sank back on the dusty red plush seat of the day-coach feeling its gritty texture against her neck, rather enjoying the queer, shabby car, so entirely American with a ' butcher ' in a white jacket selling magazines and candy and salted peanuts.

She was going away—into an unknown world, to unknown adventures. She felt free and relieved. And she kept this feeling of freedom through the morning on the train, through the trip on the rickety, open station bus in the chilly mountain air.

The old feeling of desolation, of being alone and unmated hovered just around the edge of her consciousness. But a curious delicate sense of pleasure kept it away—a feeling of expectancy, of shy, uncertain hope—the feeling of being a young girl.

PART III

PART III

Mariana found a small cottage on the edge of a little wood. A clear stream ran over rocks and pebbles almost at her door. She listened to the sound it made all the summer with never wearying pleasure. Often it murmured as if someone were whispering, but after a rain it chattered a bright babble. After heavy storms it rose and overflowed the woods and rushed through the trees loudly and menacingly.

She bathed in it every morning. She would stand naked on the bank and splash the clear water over her trembling body. Rubbed dry and warm she would sit on the steps to eat her breakfast, because it was the only place which the morning sunlight touched. A chipmunk would creep up to steal crumbs of bread ; when she ate an orange, he would pick up a pip in two tiny paws and gravely nibble it, imitating her.

The trees were full of red squirrels. They leaped from bough to bough. Two owls built a nest in the maple tree which made a roof far above the cottage roof. They sighed at each other at night. Mariana supposed it was a kind of courting.

There were silver-grey shrewmice in the grass.

233

They came into the open-air kitchen, nibbled the bread, fell in the milk and had to be rescued—like creatures in *Alice in Wonderland*, thought Mariana.

The woods were a constant delight to her. She could never tell what little wild creature would appear between the leaves. They were hardly afraid of her. The squirrels would drink from her coffee cup, almost within reach. She always hoped to see deer, and once wandering by moonlight she saw two lovely figures in the path before her. They stood looking at her as she looked at them. Then in a second, with a rustling of boughs, they were gone.

In her relief at being alone again and in her interest in the woods, she felt excited and happy. On sunny days she walked in the fields covered with large white moon-daisies with a feeling of dreamy rapture, or lay in the grass and watched some insect climbing a stalk and the red fritillaries flying from flower to flower. She wanted to feel every minute of the day, to see, to hear, to sense everything in the earth around her. She reproached herself for being dull, for having wasted days in grief and in small worries when this extraordinarily bright pageant was to be seen only by opening human eyes.

But May and June were wet that year. Day after day the grey sky dripped rain upon the house

and upon the fields and woods—a heavy unlight-
ening rain, lasting all night, all day, all night.
Then the sun came out again, dazzling bright,
glittering on the wet leaves and grasses.

Mariana had been told that sun-bathing would
be good for her. So when the sun shone most
warmly, she would take off all her clothes and
lie naked in the grass. The blades of the grass
were damp and cool against her flesh. She looked
down and saw her round, high breasts and her
strong thighs. She felt open like Danaë to the embrace of the sun—as if its rays, as in the picture
of Akhenaten, had golden hands to touch her
with. As she grew warm she felt these gilded
hands caressing, exploring all the secrets of her
body. The sunlight seemed to get in her head.
She grew dazed. Then almost frightened she
would spring up, sun-warm all over, and go back
to the cottage. Still naked, she would lie in a deck
chair where the sun fell only on her shoulders and
try to write.

Sigrid came up once for a week. It was at the
time of the artists' festival, when they gave a show
every year to raise money for charity. This year
they were giving *The Birthday of the Infanta* as a
pantomime with dancing. Mariana had been
asked to take part in it, but had refused because
it was so far to go to rehearsals.

It was the custom for all the audience to wear fancy dress. They came early to the ground, an open field in the woods, and there were merry-go-rounds and dancing in the open air and games and puppet-shows.

Mariana had seen it once before when she had first come to Edgewood with Alan, but then she had played in the pantomime. They had come just in time for her to dress, and Alan had taken her away as soon as it was over, so she had hardly seen the grounds or the crowd. She knew everyone ate dinner outdoors in the fields, cooking it over open fires, and thought it must be pretty to see the bright costumes gradually fading in the sunset, and the fires growing brighter as the darkness increased.

On the day of the festival, Mariana and Sigrid began to dress as soon as lunch was over. They had made their costumes of cheap sateen, and painted them. They were only meant to glitter for a day. Sigrid's was almond green to set off her fair straight bobbed hair and was painted with borders of gold. Mariana's was violet painted with silver flowers to imitate embroidery, with puffed sleeves of paler shades of mauve. She had braided strings of pearls in her hair and looked, Sigrid said, like an illustration from the *Mabinogion*.

236

They set off in the early afternoon to walk the three miles to the show-grounds.

Squirrels mocked them as they went through the woods and some little children on a small farm came out and gaped at them, but they did not care. They felt that they were properly dressed for the first time in their lives in the clothes that they should wear, the clothes that suitably clothed their spirits.

" Let's never wear anything else," Sigrid said. " How *can* people wear brown tweed ? It is a sin against the soul."

" I wish," said Mariana, " I could be like the young knight in the *Canterbury Pilgrims*. Do you remember Chaucer says he was ' embroidered as it were a mede'? I should like always to be as thickly embroidered with flowers as an English field. I think our clothes should blossom in the spring : in autumn they might be russet and orange like fallen leaves, and in winter I suppose white, perhaps touched with scarlet like fire and holly berries. So we would follow the course of the year and be part of the beauty of nature, till we were buried in a white shroud spotted with snowdrops to figure tears."

They came out on the edge of the show-ground. It was full of people in fancy costume talking and laughing. A comic boxing match was going on in one corner, and in another a tiny merry-go-round was being turned by hand while beside it a sculptor they knew, dressed in rags, played a hand organ, his little son dressed as a monkey begging for pennies from the crowd.

" How pretty it is," said Sigrid; " I am so glad we came." They saw Mariana's old friend, William Hervey, who always helped to organise the shows, dressed as a devil.

" When did you become a devil? " Sigrid asked. " I thought you were living still. Or are you appearing, like us, for the first time in your true colours ? "

"That is it," said Hervey, "I am really a very wicked man."

" ' He was a very wicked man,' " Mariana quoted, " ' but very good to me. If you called a dog Hervey I should love it ! ' "

" I shan't," Hervey answered. " I shall call myself Hervey instead."   And he bowed smiling before her.

They went to a Punch and Judy show which was beginning, and after it was over danced with young men they knew on the green.

The clear sky grew streaked with red ribbons of sunset, here and there, one by one, glowing spots appeared in the field and thin bluish spires of smoke rose palely against the darkening woods.

The two girls found the fire of the friend who had invited them to dinner. They helped to bring dry brushwood and set the coffee-pot in a secure place over the flames, buried potatoes in the ashes and roasted strips of pumpkin by the hot coals. It was charming. The darkening field and the little glowing fires, voices calling, someone singing in the distance, dogs barking on a distant farm. Mariana was almost too happy in these impressions to talk or eat.

But very gradually she noticed that everything was changing. Everyone had brought thermos bottles of iced cocktails and jugs of rum and applejack. Everyone was drinking. Everyone was getting drunk. The voices grew louder, people shouted hoarsely to one another. There were loud shouts of laughter, yells and cat-calls.

Mariana and Sigrid, looking about them as dinner went on, saw people getting drunker and drunker. A famous painter was roaring drunk and shouting at the hillside, which shouted back mockingly.

The other girls of their party were flushed with drink. One was dressed as an oread, her wreath of leaves had slipped over one ear and her make-up had run so that her face was red and blotchy. She was lying on the shoulder of a young man she did not care for in sober hours. He slipped one hand in her breast and under her loose tunic began to explore further. Her husband sitting on the other side of the fire paid no attention, he was engaged with a girl he had met for the first time that evening. They were both quite drunk, and presently they got up and went off to the woods. They appeared again much later, cold, dishevelled and querulous, having slept off both drunkenness and desire.

Mariana and Sigrid were amazed ; they had seen drinking at parties in New York, but nothing like this. They drew a little away to one side of the fire.

A group of people came up dressed as Bacchus and his crew, dragging a small stubborn donkey by a gilded rope. Mariana's purple dress caught the eye of Bacchus who was their ringleader, a well-known painter, very large and very drunk, his grey curls crowned with ivy leaves.

" It is the Queen of the Gods," he said, swaying before Mariana. " She must drink with us, and bless our revels."

He had a half-empty bottle of gin in his hand, which he extended towards her. She refused to drink—politely, as if he was sober. She disliked the raw fiery liquor, and was disgusted at the idea of drinking from the bottle-mouth which they had all been lipping.

" The Queen will not drink with us," Bacchus

said, sadly turning towards his crew who had scattered into a wide circle and were teasing the donkey by throwing fire crackers under its hooves. It kicked violently and occasionally caught one of them with its heels. Then all the rest cheered and roared with laughter.

" The Goddess is *not* favourable to our revels ! " Bacchus shouted. " We must pour a libation to her," and he suddenly tilted up the bottle and poured it over Mariana's head. She sprang up indignantly, too angry to speak. And he retreated, mumbling some apology. His crew followed, the donkey getting in a shrewd kick on someone's leg, and with shouts of laughter drowning the curses of the injured man they trooped away.

Sigrid began trying to dry Mariana's hair and the neck of her dress which reeked of the raw gin.

" Let's go away," she said. " It's horrible."

"Let's stay for the show, anyway," Mariana said, still trembling with shock and annoyance, but half amused by Bacchus and his revellers.

They did stay, and the pantomime was very good, with beautiful dancing and music by the artists who gave their services. But the audience was a great nuisance, shouting and stamping and cat-calling in the midst of the action, falling asleep, or drunkenly wandering on to the stage.

241

The performers always making the best of it and going on as if nothing were happening.

As Sigrid and Mariana returned through the fair-grounds late that night in the broad white moonlight, they passed the ashes of their camp-fire and found two of their party still there, lying heavily asleep in the wet grass.

" Shall we try to wake them or cover them up ? " Mariana said.

" I shouldn't bother," Sigrid said indifferently. She did not care in the least whether they died of pneumonia or not, and was frank enough to show it.

But on the way home she began to cry.

" It should have been so gay," she said. " And it was so ugly."

After Sigrid left, Mariana felt her loneliness more acutely. The old impression of being thwarted returned to her. She felt again, as she had felt before she was married, that life went by like a brightly coloured pilgrimage on some other road, hidden from her by thickets, while she stayed on alone in the woods not knowing where to go. She felt she must go out, must seek for what she wanted (and what was it ?) and did not know what to do or where to go. And again she felt the warm tides of her blood beat against the walls of her veins as if she were herself imprisoning them.

She often thought of her marriage and of Alan. He had been up to see her three or four times. But he was on the staff of a newspaper now, and the journey was so long and the time he could spend so short that he had given up coming. She was not really sorry. She had such a keen feeling of something wrong. It grew upon her—a feeling of being in the wrong world. When he came up to see her and they ate their dinner in the open-air dining-room with the squirrels chattering over their heads, and Alan, tired out with his journey, had gone to sleep after embracing her, she would lie thinking how sweet it would have been if she could have accepted him wholly, given herself to his life unrestrainedly without doubt and misgiving. And she felt again that she was in danger. She was in the wrong place with the wrong man.

She knew that her real break with Alan had happened when she left him. These last few meetings were like the creepers of a vine still clinging when the bough which held them had been cut away. They had to be broken one by one. But it was all over. They could not hold her any more. These few last embraces were the expiring force of the instinct that had brought them together— the last movements of habit. Alan was not coming up to see her any more. He still took it for granted apparently that she would return to him in the fall ; but she knew that she would not. It was no longer necessary to tell him so now that they did not see one another.

Once he had come with a present of a small Maltese kitten. It was a kitten of Lucio Ferrano's cat, Falada, and had been born and suckled under the dangling feet of Don Quixote and Orlando Furioso. Mariana called it Cinderella because it was the most beautiful blue grey like the ashes of black paper, and also because *Cinderella* was the first play she had seen Ferrano's puppets give. It was called Cindy in the end in memory of a kind cook her grandmother had had, and it became a great pleasure and diversion to her. It slept on her shoulder at night, under the fall of her hair, purring in a tiny way like a little far-off sea. If it went to sleep she would tease it and stroke it awake until it began again its minute rhythms, and she would fall asleep in its little waves of sound with the wider sound of the brook around them.

But the summer was passing. Mariana could see how the green of the leaves was changing, growing yellower and warmer. The Michaelmas daisies were beginning to bloom in the fields of golden rod.

The summer is over, she thought sadly, and

nothing happened. Of course there is something wrong with me. There must be or I would not have had this particular life. I invite it. I should never marry again, even if I could, she thought inconsequently. In marriage you are at the mercy of another person. You do things you would never do if you were free. I do not think that it is marriage that is wrong, it is the people who marry. They demand something of marriage that is not marriage : they take advantage through it. It is a trap because you are in it with an illiberal and mean personality and are yourself narrow and suspicious. We are all so. People who were truly good would not think of it as a trap at all, and so they would not make it so. But as people are, I do not want to be married.

She realised in herself depth beyond depth of distrust of the world and of the people in it, of her own power to be content or to make others happy. She wanted to fight clear of responsibility, of being involved again in some unhappy communion. And yet she was lonely, and wished for a companion. In spite of Cindy, the nights frightened her and the rainy days depressed her.

I must make the best of it, must live through it, she thought. But living is a long thing, and I am afraid. She had grown honestly to admit that her life was now an unhappy one.

September was passing—the leaves were beginning to turn. Here and there a leaf was delicately edged with red, a bough paling to yellow.

It is autumn, Mariana thought. My summer has gone already. Summer, life, love seemed to be leaving her together.

One night when the maple tree above the house was growing pink and flame coloured she left the cottage and started to walk through the fields and dark woods beyond her little wood. A thin red line of sunset was still in the sky as she brushed through the golden rod in the fields, but when she entered the woods again, the thick-growing trees hid it. She could only see the clear, cold sky with the first stars beginning to shine out. She was going to dinner with a friend who lived two miles away beyond the woods—a dark Irish girl married to a sculptor, very poor, and settled in a small farmhouse. Mariana liked her without knowing her very well. There was something tragic and sweet in her manner and in the way that she looked out of her large black eyes.

Mariana went rapidly through the woods ; little as she feared wandering alone, she did not want the darkness to catch her under the trees. She found herself hurrying and laughed at her fears. There is nothing in these woods, she told herself, nothing to be afraid of. What if that should be a bear you hear walking at the side of the road ? It won't hurt you—at least it most probably won't. You have to take some chances. Now you think you hear a large rattlesnake gliding by. You must decide which you prefer. You can't have both a rattlesnake and a bear. It's entirely too improbable.

She came out from under the last trees into open fields. Far ahead to the right she could see the tiny twinkling light of the farmhouse to which she was going and she left the road, knowing there was a path, but could not find it in the growing darkness. The briars and the golden rod caught at her thin skirts of flowered silk, her bare ankles and plaited sandals. It is autumn, she thought. I am a strayed reveller from summer in these clothes. My time is over. It is cold and the leaves are falling. She had almost forgotten her commonplace journey to dinner with an acquaintance.

A chilly wind had sprung up. The light was still far ahead of her. She struggled on through the thick growth of the field, and then through a marshy spot where the water from the weeds ran cold and wet into her summer sandals. But she hurried on in the dark, caught by briars and delayed by bushes with the light growing closer until in a few minutes more she came on to clear ground. The rays from the window streamed out

247

into the darkness and lit the grass before her. She looked down at her feet, stained and damp. I am not fit to go into a house, she thought, I shall get the rugs wet. Reluctant to leave the darkness she stood looking up to the sky, black now and full of stars. A figure passing by the window caught her eye. It was her friend, Molly Byrne, laying the table. Then a man's form moved by : then another man passed. I must go in, she thought, and not stand here in the night staring ; it must be late. But she lingered still, unwilling to face the lights and the greetings and happy in the secrecy of the darkness.

With an effort she moved to the door and lifted the knocker. Molly Byrne came out. Her dark head rose from a swirl of white organdie like a delicate ruff in an old painting. " Come in, Mariana," she said, " it is cold."

The strange simplicity of her greeting was like the voice of the night. As they entered the one room, Mariana's eyes, adjusted to darkness, were dazzled by the light of the great log fire and of the candles on the table and bookshelf.

John Swenson, the sculptor, came to meet her. He was a powerful, taciturn Swede with a heavy fair head. Behind him she saw another man, smaller and also fair, dressed in riding-breeches and a shooting-jacket.

248

" This is my friend, John Holworth," Swenson said in his heavy accent. " And this is Miss Clare," he added as an afterthought.

She smiled at this stranger. He smiled back at her and she noticed that his eyebrows and eyelashes were as yellow as his hair, and gilded now with firelight.

" But you are wet, Miss Clare," Swenson said. " You will catch a cold. You must change your shoes and stockings. Molly, Miss Clare is wet."

" I don't need to change, really," said Mariana hurriedly. " I never do," she added truthfully, " and it never hurts me. I'll dry them here by the fire."

Molly stood beside her, not urging her to change, delicately waiting to know her will.

She smiled at Molly, relieved not to be urged, and stretched her slim feet to the blaze. She noticed that John Holworth looked at her intently, saying nothing, almost as if he were trying to recognise her. At length he smiled and began to talk with them, while Molly moved silently about the room, setting on the painted pine table the green glass from Woolworth's and the cheap pretty English china, bringing in a casserole containing a rabbit Swenson had shot, and vegetables they had grown themselves, a jug of

249

cider from the next farm and a dish of apples from the tree by the back door.

They had a pleasant evening and Mariana liked John Holworth. He seemed rather gentle and well-bred, and without being particularly intelligent or well educated was interesting because he observed the world around him so closely. She discovered that he was a lieutenant in the infantry and had been stationed in the Philippines. She liked him when he spoke of the natives. He seemed really to appreciate them. He had just left the Islands and was on his way to a new post. "Where are you going ? " she asked.

" To Texas," he answered with a slight groan. " You get sent to the most horrible places when you are in the army. You make friends and have to leave them."

" Why do you stay in the army, Jack ? " asked Swenson. " You can't really like such a life."

" I stay in it," Holworth said frankly, " because it's the only thing in the world I'm fit for. I'm really uneducated, except for some knowledge of mathematics. I loathe business of any description. I have no money and not the energy or intelligence to master a profession now. I couldn't teach, except perhaps in primary schools, because I have no degrees. You know my father was so anxious to have me go into the army because he and my grandfather were army men that I thought I should go as I was his only son. Now he's dead I'd leave it, but I don't know what else to do. There's nothing I really want to do, and almost all of my friends are in the army—naturally, for I was brought up in it. I feel at home in it. And yet I don't really like the life. It is so purposeless. Day in and day out I do the same thing. In time of peace it all seems to amount to nothing, and I'm not fool enough to wish for a war."

Mariana felt something unaroused and listless in his personality. Yet his body was singularly swift and accurate in small motions. His grey eyes took them all in like the eyes of an intelligent animal, and caught their least movement or change of expression. But the quick interest of the eye lacked the control of a central interest. She felt sorry for him.

When she rose to go he said he would walk home with her, and added that it was not much out of his way; he was staying at a farmhouse on the other side of the woods. They started out together in the clear, chilly night.

He scarcely spoke as they found their way down the narrow path that Mariana had missed; but when they were walking on the road, she realised that he was trying to see her face and heard him speaking in a reminiscent voice.

" And can you really be Mariana Clare ? " he was saying. She turned to him in surprise. " And you don't remember me at all ? I was waiting to see. I did hope you would remember me. But you don't."

" No," she said, " I am sorry. Should I remember you ? When did we meet ? Was it long ago ? "

" You were flying a kite," he said. " Do you remember now ? "

" Were you the boy who came with Hal that day ? I never knew your name."

" Yes," he answered, " I was the boy who came with Hal—— And you were Mariana Clare. I've remembered you all these years. I think I would have known you even if they hadn't told me your name. You haven't changed in the least."

She could tell by his voice that he was smiling.

" I think I must have changed a little, I was only twelve."

" You were only twelve, and it is ten years ago. I was trying to remember at dinner how many years it was."

" It is a long time," said Mariana.

" Yes," he said, " it was too long. I meant to come back years ago to see if you still flew a kite on the beach by the palmettos. But I went to school just then and while I was away my father was transferred to another post. And anyway, you have left. Do you ever fly kites now ? "

" No," she said gravely. It was sad to think that she would never again be that child who still played on a lonely beach in John Holworth's memory.

My grandmother is dead, she thought. Hal is dead. This stranger is perhaps the only white person in the world, the only person, may be, except old Maum' Hester and her children, who remembers that child.

She looked at him gratefully. He had given that child the boon of a brief mortal immortality.

Holworth came to see Mariana often in the following days. He was pleased and touched to find in this rather frail lonely girl the child he remembered playing alone by the Southern shore.

It is as if I had met Annabelle Lee, he thought— that was what came into my mind, I remember, when we found her under the palmettos with a tiny Chinese bird-kite.

I was a child and she was a child
In that kingdom by the sea.

He found himself against his will becoming more and more attracted to her. He did not like it, because she was married, and even if she had been unmarried he did not see how he could have taken her to live in a small house on an army post in Texas with his jealous, difficult mother on a second lieutenant's pay. And he could hardly think of having a casual affair with a young woman whom he remembered as a child.

It is because you remember her as a child and identify her still with that child that you are so attracted to her, his honest mind told him. Where have you read in a book lately that most men would marry child slaves if they could have the secret desire of their hearts? Girls attract you most—you know it—before they are fit to be married at all, at fourteen or fifteen. Mariana attracts you so much because she is decently grown up, has even been married so that your desires are possible and lawful, and yet you can think of her still as a child who could be raped—without really hurting her.

One day his thoughts of her and the excitement of his body troubled him so much that in restless agitation he sprang from the grass where he had been lying. I'll go and see John, he thought, and go swimming with him in the pool. It's wicked that my body should behave like this at the mere thought of Mariana.

*　　*　　*

254

Mariana lying on her couch had been thinking of John Holworth. But her thoughts were not sensual ones at all. I do like him, she thought. It is as if someone had come from another world to talk to me of the past, of Hal and the Island. He even thinks he remembers Cindy and Maum' Hester and her children, and Hal's dog, Cæsar. Think of meeting someone here who remembers how Cæsar chased fish in the pools the sea left, and never caught them! And he is very kind to me. He behaves as if he thought of me as a child still.

The heat of the sun falling on her body made her restless. I will go to see Molly and swim in the pool, she thought. She took her bathing suit and a light coat, put on a shady straw hat and started to walk down the field.

As she came out into the road she saw Jack Holworth ahead of her. His quick ears caught her step, and he turned and came back to meet her.

" Were you going to swim at Molly's," he asked, seeing the bathing suit over her arm.

" Yes," she said, noticing his.

" I was, too."

They walked on together. The cold water of the river refreshed them. Molly and John Swenson were not at home, but when they had dressed after swimming and were leaving again, they met them returning through the field with a rabbit Swenson had shot and a basket of apples.

"But you must stay to supper," Swenson answered to all their attempted refusals. "It is a hot night and you are here. If you have no engagements you must stay."

They all went into the farmhouse room and Mariana set the table while Molly cooked the supper, and Swenson and Holworth sat by the empty hearth talking and sipping their glasses of cider. The night was oppressively hot, though it was October.

They sat late talking, and Mariana and Jack Holworth walked back together through the woods. It was so black that they could hardly stay upon the road. Constantly one or the other would stray to the side and feel the thick weeds against their ankles warning them that they were going astray.

It was still hot and the air was heavy, and before they left the forest thunder began to roll about the horizon and sudden flashes of lightning outlined the black woods. Dazzling sheet lightning lit the field as they approached Mariana's cottage. They could see every blossom of golden rod in its unnatural glare.

"You must come in until this is over," Mariana said, "you will be killed." They climbed the steps and entered the studio. Terrific thunder seemed to roll after them and Mariana hastily shut the door. She felt as if she were shutting it against some monster and could not be sure that the door would keep it out. The cottage was intensely black except when the lightning flashed. By its fitful glare she tried to find the matches, and could not. " Have you any matches ? " she asked Holworth. " I can't find them." He felt in all his pockets.

" I can't find any, either," he said. " I must have left them on the table at Swenson's. I remember lighting my pipe just before we started."

Mariana went on searching about the room for matches. At last she felt the sharp oblong shape of a match-box, and relieved, picked it up. It was empty. A tremendous roar of thunder began, as if the universe broke about their ears. Mariana gave a stifled cry. Holworth groped towards her in the darkness and found her hand.

" Sit down on the couch, Mariana," he said, " it will be over soon. That was the worst, I think."

He led her to the couch and they sat down together. He could feel that she was trembling slightly. He put his arm around her and held her quietly. She did not draw back. She felt a simple

257

feeling of comfort and confidence at this human nearness.

But in Jack Holworth all the desire of the past weeks seemed to be rising, burning. He felt the lift of his body. He was in the hot dark on a bed with this girl. He wanted her. He put his hand on her hair, and she did not move. She was half in a dream, tired and frightened of the storm, safe inside his warm arm.

But Holworth could not control himself any longer. All the desire of barren months, all his more recent desire for Mariana seemed to have come together at this point, to blaze in his mind until conscious thought went out. He crushed Mariana to him. She was frightened and tried to draw away. The soft twisting of her body thrilled his flesh pressing against it. He pressed her down on the couch, kissing her, pulling aside her clothes.

" Oh, no, no," she whispered. " Oh, no, please don't, please don't."

She did not struggle any more, only feebly with her hands she tried to keep him away from the centre he was seeking. She did not cry out. He would have stopped if she had. He took her silence partly as consent. She did not struggle because she was afraid of struggling. It seemed to her more terrible than letting him have his way.

And soon he had it. But as she felt his body she

trembled with apprehension, with fear of the unknown, more frightened, more shocked than she had been in that first embrace when she had been a virgin.

The thunder was over and it had begun quietly to rain. Holworth's lust had been succeeded by a profound tenderness. Mariana seemed infinitely dear to him, like his own child. He leaned over her, kissing her bare shoulders and her hair. In the confusion of his senses it seemed to him that the rain must be falling on her face, for her cheeks were wet against his lips. Instinctively, he leaned over her to protect her body from the storm. It was only later that he realised that her face was wet with tears.

He left her unwillingly early in the morning, and she finally went to bed in the inner bedroom and lay sadly listening to the falling rain until it turned into a rain of sleep.

*　　*　　*

When Holworth came to see Mariana the next day, he was anxious and uncomfortable ; he was afraid that she would look at him with dislike or reproach in her eyes. At the farmhouse where he stayed he tried to buy some chrysanthemums to take her. But the woman of the house, as old as his grandmother, refused to sell them, and gave him a large bunch of white and pink ones and all sorts of old-fashioned garden flowers as well.

" Are you going to see Miss Clare ? " she asked with a twinkle not dimmed by age, " she's a sweet, pretty young lady, but she doesn't look stout. She's terrible delicate, I'm afraid."

" I'm afraid she's not strong," he said uncomfortably. He wished he had been a young lover, going to see the avowed object of his love on the way to engagement and marriage in a country church with the good wishes of the country people. He disliked this illicit relationship, which, if it went further, might bring trouble on Mariana. I must be very careful, he thought, not to do anything to cause talk. I was an animal last night. How could I have behaved so ? What a fool I was to think she wanted me to embrace her ! Not that I doubt she wants to be embraced. She's young. But she wasn't expecting a sudden attack. Why I almost ravished her ! Now she is probably completely disgusted with me. Things can never be the same again.

His step faltered. He was unwilling to go on. But I must go, he thought. Mariana wouldn't understand it. I don't know what she might not think if I stayed away. He walked through the last field and approached the house. She was reading on the porch and came down to meet him. The kitten with exaggerated fear ran up a tree and hung staring till Mariana picked it off like a chestnut burr. They laughed.

Mariana behaved precisely as if nothing had happened. The afternoon was warm and she was sitting in the sun in a sleeveless frock and a shady straw hat. It seemed as if everything were precisely the same. Holworth felt relieved and at the same time baffled, for the sight of Mariana's slim arms warmed and coloured by the sun and the look of her breasts rounding under the tight bodice of her frock began to agitate him as soon as his concern over her was a little relieved by her quiet, cheerful manner.

" You feel all right to-day ? " he asked still troubled.

" Yes, very well," she said calmly, but rather hurriedly, changing the subject. " I met a red fox in the path when I went for water before breakfast. Such a pretty thing, as red as flame and it had such a secret look."

" What did it do ? " he asked. She is evading me, he thought. She is pretending nothing has happened between us. It means she does not like me. I must pretend too.

" It slipped away through the trees like light, without any sound."

They talked casually. Mariana asked him to stay to dinner and went downstairs to make a salad. He followed and helped her.

They ate dinner in the out-door dining-room, though it was cold in the woods with the last light of sunset shining behind the trees. When they had finished—and neither of them ate much—they went up to the studio and built a fire of boughs. They sat talking. It was a black, moonless night with sharp stars glittering in the cold. Holworth took Mariana's hand. "Mariana, let me love you," he said. She drew back. "I will not hurt you, I will only kiss you." She moved away slightly, unwilling. He started back, his nerves quivering. She dislikes me, he thought, I have disgusted her. Mariana realised what he was thinking and laid her hand on his.

"*No, no,*" she said, distressed to think that he would feel she disliked his touch. She took his hand and smiled at him. He bent and kissed her. She let him kiss her and hold her in his arm, but was unwilling that he should proceed to more intimate love-making. She did not want him to, her body shrank away from him. And in the end it was only to keep him from being hurt by her unwillingness, because she was afraid that he might think he had been repulsive to her, that she allowed him to embrace her.

She never learned to take pleasure in his embraces. She liked and she was comforted by the warmth of his passion and the tenderness of his caresses. But he was not skilled in making love as Alan had been. The strength of his desire and his youth carried him away. His embraces were sudden and too soon over. She was hardly stirred by them, and so she felt no pain or trouble afterwards. Then his tenderness enveloped her, and she felt secure and protected as a child with an elder brother. She would go to sleep inside his arms with a great content, feeling for a few hours safe from loneliness and even from approaching age and death.

" Will you get a divorce and marry me ? " he sometimes asked her against his better judgment.

" No," she always said smiling. " We don't really want to marry each other."

He would be sorry and yet relieved, for he did not see how they could be married and was not sure that they would be happy together. Mariana knew that she did not care for him at all as a lover, but was fond of him as of a favourite cousin. His love-making was nothing to her apart from the pleasure it gave him. She would rather not have been embraced, though she had got over her first shock and instinctive recoil.

I have committed adultery, she thought, how

strange that is, and how strange that I should feel nothing about it at all ! I suppose that whatever you do seems perfectly natural to you because you are doing it and are in it. It becomes the condition under which you live. There are so many things I could never have believed would happen to me in my life. But it all seemed natural enough at the time ; you come so gradually down these odd paths that you do not realise where you are until you are already accustomed to being there.

She knew their association could not last. There were only four weeks left of Holworth's leave and at the end of them he must go to the army post in Texas. They could not see each other again for at least a year : they might never meet again—it was only an interlude in her life. He was very charming, but their association did not really affect her much. She stood outside it, still essentially solitary and unmated, and when Holworth was not there to divert her, often melancholy and lonely.

The four weeks were drawing to a close. October was wonderfully clear and warm that year, only the yellow leaves, falling, falling in the windless air told them that the winter was at hand. Mariana knew it and yet her fancy could not believe it. The air was so still and golden that it seemed this weather might last for ever, that the charm of the autumn could never be broken.

Holworth's character, open and sweet-natured if naturally rather feckless, became really dear to her. In the hours when he was not bent on making love, he was a gay and kind companion. He loved fishing, and together they explored all the streams nearby. On many mornings he would come for her just after breakfast, and they would walk through the woods to some stream. Lying on the grass she would read *The Compleat Angler* and watch Holworth casting his line, for she did not care to fish. When the fish would not bite or he grew tired of tempting them, she read Walton aloud to him until their minds were full of clear streams running and the sound of brooks. She thought that his pleasure in Walton, whom he had never read before, was very natural because his own nature seemed simple and sweet, a little shallow and light perhaps, but bright and clean and gay like the streams Cotton had fished in.

The days went by, day after day of clear, yellow weather. The bronze and brazen leaves hung in the windless air like the leaves on the trees of the Golden Wood and the Copper Wood in the fairy tale. The days went by one after another as if they would never change and never end. And quite suddenly they realised that there were only two days left of his leave.

Holworth felt real distress. The thought of leaving Mariana alone in the woods depressed him. He was afraid that she might suffer with the coming cold, or might grow ill or might fall and hurt herself in the woods on some dark night with no one to help her, and no one but the kitten to notice she had not come home. He begged her to go back to New York, but she refused to go and he had no alternative to suggest. For himself he felt pain at leaving her, pain that this charming holiday was over. But Mariana had wounded his masculine pride by her indifference to his embraces. She had been gentle, responsive, tender, anxious that he should be happy. But he realised that her body had had no thrilling pleasure from his and guessed that it had not always been so, that with Alan her body had been awakened to delight. He felt that she must be so profoundly indifferent to him that his wildest caresses left her untouched, and that somehow as a lover he was a failure. It was an uncomfortable feeling. It kept his love for Mariana from developing as it might have. It remained a tenderness for a remembered child, a friendship with a charming character. It could not develop further.

Mariana found that she was not really sorry that

he was going. Their association had been sweet, but it had been for her an unnatural condition. She had let Holworth, for whom she had only felt friendliness, make love to her. It had been wrong for her to do so because she had not loved him. It had only been a refuge and a respite from the loneliness of her life. But she was conscious of a certain feeling of relief and of gratitude towards him. He had finally broken the bond that had held her to Alan. His body had destroyed the particularity of her association with Alan. She was no longer peculiarly his. He would not even want her back if he knew of this, and she would certainly never return to him without telling him about it. Her bondage was over.

And what freedom had she won? The right to live alone—rather poorly—to be made casual and irresponsible love to by anyone she would let have her. Her association with Holworth had spoiled the feeling of expectancy she had kept all through the summer even when she was most lonely. This was not what she wanted. She realised now what her life would probably be. Love for her would not be the strong growing thing she had once hoped for—strong enough, growing, developing, changing—to last a lifetime, a sort of blood kinship that would not fail when lust began to chill. It would be something very different, a casual friendship informed with passion for a time and not to last : she would regard it as a holiday from the loneliness of living until perhaps approaching age put an end to her attractiveness. She could not believe that there would be anything better for her in life than that. She felt afraid and distrustful, like an animal separated from its own kind and unable to mate.

The day on which Holworth had to leave came at last. The enchantment was broken : the windless calm that had lasted for over a month came to an end. Dark clouds were blown across the sky all day. No drops fell, but the wind roared in the trees and the bright leaves came raining down. They had said their real good-bye the night before. It had been said by their bodies. Now on the station platform waiting for the train, they listened to the groaning of the trees bending in the wind, smiled at each other and had no more to say.

Coming back from the station in the car that had taken them there Mariana stopped to buy some vegetables in the town. As she stood hesitating outside a shop window looking at a basket of purple grapes, a man came up to her.

John Linschoten was a man she had known for several years. Before she had been married, he had sometimes come to see her and had been rather attracted by her ; but as she had not seemed even to realise it, he had been discouraged and had never shown his interest more plainly. He was a tall, sandy-haired young man, ten or twelve years older than Mariana. His clear aquiline features were rather handsome and aristocratic. He was strong and well-built, but thin and a little stiff. It was the outward appearance of his rather cold, reserved nature.

Now he came up to Mariana and asked her if she would come to dinner with him. She considered a moment, but there was no reason why she could not come—there was no one waiting for her at the cottage. The kitten would only play a little later in the woods; it had a bowl of milk, so it would not be thirsty or hungry. She said, therefore, that she would come, and dismissed the car. Since she was going to save a few cents at least by dining out, she went back into the shop and bought the purple grapes, and coming out into the village street with the dust blowing and the wind catching at her coat, climbed into his battered runabout, beside him; and they drove through the windy late afternoon to his house.

He accompanied her to the door before putting the car away. His Japanese servant, Toru, came out smiling a welcome and took her coat and hat and put her by the fire.

The big table behind her was covered with

sheets of paper, and she saw mathematical symbols on them.

"Master always work, study, write book," said Toru apologetically, but evidently proud of the papers. He touched them lightly, putting them in better order without altering their arrangement. Linschoten had told her that Toru was working and saving money and learning English at the same time in order to go to an American university, and that he had now set his heart on studying physics under Linschoten himself and meant to wait till he went back to teaching.

Meanwhile Linschoten coached him a little and lent him books and discussed what he read with him. The young man had become his protégé, but remained at the same time an excellent servant who quietly did the entire work of the small house from making the fires to arranging the flowers. Now he went out and brought in another log. Kneeling beside Mariana he put a footstool at her feet. "Miss Clare perhaps stool her feet," he said; smiled when she accepted and disappeared as Linschoten came in.

The dinner that Toru set for them was delicious, there was white wine glowing in the long-stemmed glasses and candles shining in the silver candlesticks, the fire leaped hotly up the chimney to drive the cold away.

After dinner they sat by the fire talking. It was a pleasant evening, Mariana had almost forgotten that Holworth had gone away that afternoon. As she looked in the leaping fire, she was conscious of a certain secret sense of relief, of a delicate stirring, as if that lost feeling of expectancy and wonder might return if she could only be very still and wait.

When Linschoten drove her back to her cottage the night was glittering with cold stars, the wind had blown the clouds away ; but on the earth the roads were soft with the thick fall of leaves.

After that evening they spent many others together, sometimes at Linschoten's house, sometimes at Mariana's. They borrowed each other's books and read each other's writing. Mariana could not understand his book on physics, though she listened with interest when he talked about it. But he had some appreciation of her poetry.

November went by, and December, while their friendship advanced by slow degrees. The Indian Summer was so warm that Mariana still ate many meals out-doors. A few dry leaves hung here and there on the branches. But all the small creatures in the wood seemed to have gone to bed : she never saw them again.

Her friendly feeling for Linschoten had always had a deep foundation because she had discovered when she met him that he remembered her father. As a little boy he had been taken South for a month after some child's illness, and his father had brought letters to hers as had so many Northern visitors because Clare had been at a Northern university. Linschoten remembered Captain Clare riding a roan horse up to the door, and remembered going to the plantation to spend the day and being taken up in front of him on to the saddle for a ride down the avenue. This had been before Mariana was born. She could not remember her father or her mother at all. She often asked Linschoten to tell her the story again.

This childish memory gave Mariana a special lustre in Linschoten's eyes, because he thought of her as belonging to an aristocracy, and of having come to her present position by the fall as it were of a dynasty, like some unhappy lady of old time. Their friendship was a quiet, almost old-fashioned one, strange in these hills where affairs often began over a week-end and ended as suddenly. They exchanged quiet visits and entertained one another at dinner, lent books and talked about them. He brought her flowers from Kingston, and delicate foods and flower-made wines prepared by Toru. Except that she went alone to his house, a friendship between their grandparents could hardly have been more decorous.

Linschoten came of an old New York Dutch family, but had been brought up in New Haven where his father had been professor of physics. He had shared his father's interests, and was now a very brilliant scholar in the same field. He had married, when still very young, a clever, pretty young Society girl. Her self-assurance and rather conscious charm had begun to bore him before a year of marriage was over. She found him unresponsive to her, and was irritated and agitated because it seemed that her charm had somehow failed. She finally left him and returned to her rather doting mother and father and to a life of casual Society contacts and constant parties with her old friends. There was no open breach between them, and Linschoten visited her often ; but first a trip that she made round the world with her parents, and then his retiring to the mountains to work quietly at his book made a convenient excuse for a virtual separation. When they met, she launched herself at his reserve, demanding something he would not or could not give, hurt herself, hurt him, and retired in angry frustration for a time, but could not let him alone. He often wished that they had never met. How could people so unsuitable be tricked into marrying ? He answered her bitter letters with cold politeness and after a little she almost ceased to write. At the

273

time when he met Mariana he had not seen his wife for nearly a year.

He felt disgusted with marriage, even with women. He thought that he should never have been so involved and was ashamed of himself for marrying unsuitably, or, once married, for not having been able to manage the situation. An old distrust of his powers to deal with life returned to him.

His shyness and this distrust of women were largely resolved in Mariana's presence by her gentleness and lack of any power of aggression. He felt as if a long attack had suddenly ceased. The garrison could put up arms, could lie in the grass and sleep. There was no longer any danger.

He was not very attracted to her physically, though he had always been aware of her beauty. Perhaps his pretty, young wife had moved him more deeply than his outraged mind had allowed him to know. And the rankling pain he still felt when he thought of her may have been the trouble of his body even more than of his mind.

But Mariana's quietness was very delightful to him. A certain quaint learning she had acquired in her solitary childhood with so many old books on the shelves, and such long winter evenings in which to read them, amused and pleased him. He regarded her as a charming individual rather than as a beautiful woman. Perhaps it was a little because they were both married still. And while he had had affairs with women of one sort and another since he had been separated from his wife, he did not think of Mariana as the kind of person with whom you have a casual affair.

But on these winter nights when Toru piled the wood high on the andirons and the fire leaped fiercely up the chimney, when Mariana sitting in the warmth of the blaze would lay aside her Paisley shawl and her bare, round arms and the soft flesh of her shoulders would glow in the fire and candle light as if painted by Titian, Linschoten, from looking at her simply with æsthetic appreciation, would gradually become aware that his heart was beating faster, and that he felt drawn to lay his hand on the soft flesh of those bare arms and to feel with fingers and with lips the white flesh of her neck, where he could see the breasts beginning to swell at the edge of her frock. And he wondered with a warm shock to his senses what, when the arms were round and soft, the thighs were like, so demurely hidden beneath full long silken skirts.

One night as she sat on the couch before his fire, her feet on a footstool, her whole body relaxed and a little sleepy, Linschoten came and sat beside her and drew close to her as if unconsciously drawn. It was a cold, windy, stormy night.

"I wish I didn't have to take you home to-night, Mariana," he said. "It will be a wild night in the woods with only a kitten for company. It seems a pity that I have to take you back."

Mariana smiled at him and their eyes met in a secret awareness, a look of half alarmed, half smiling complicity before their glances fell again.

Some night, Mariana thought, he will ask me to climb those steps with him up to his bed. If I go, the steps will creak and the wind cry after us as we climb. And what will happen afterwards, I do not know.

She felt excitement and romance in the air. But she was not ready, she was still half afraid. She drew back.

"I must go home," she said. "I shall not be afraid in the woods. The kitten always sleeps with me and the wind blows me to sleep. Do you re-member that child's story *At the Back of the North Wind*? How the little boy sleeps in the stable over the horses and hears them eating and stamping below as he lies in the loft with the north wind blowing outside, and feels so safe and secret closed in by the hay. I always feel like that on windy nights."

She drew her shawl closely about her, and went to the fireplace, smiling at him as she warmed her hands before the blaze. Reluctantly he went to get their coats.

*   *   *

It was very cold as the winter set in, but no snow fell, and Mariana managed to keep warm by always having great fires in the studio. She still cooked downstairs in the open air, and the cold pinched her fingers as she peeled the vegetables or washed the lettuce till she could hardly use them. She put her meals on a tray when they were ready and took them up to the studio fire where she thawed her fingers and her feet which were half frozen from standing on the flags of the open-air kitchen.

Breakfast and tea were best. She had only to put a kettle on the studio fire for the tea or coffee and make toast at it. Washing dishes in the cold was the great hardship and the only thing she really minded.

But it was hard to get enough firewood. The farmers were busy about other things and thought it scarcely worth their time to cut it. Sometimes for a day or two she ran out of wood entirely. Then she went into the forest to get broken boughs or old rotten logs. The kitten went with her, taking these expeditions as a new and delightful game, hiding behind trees and rushing out to attack her or scudding outspread up large trunks, like a grey squirrel.

The evenings she spent at Linschoten's house gave her comfort as well as pleasure. While she lay back in deep chairs, someone else, the silent smiling Toru or Linschoten himself, piled heavy logs on the fire and Toru prepared the good dinner, whose dirty dishes she would not have to wash.

And she was companioned. There was someone with her who was interested to some extent at least in what she had been doing and what she had read or written. Someone to talk to and to listen to. He taught her to play chess, and though she never learned to play well, enjoyed their games played on a table before the fire with old chessmen of ivory and coral which had belonged to his great grandfather. He liked to see Mariana's face bent over the pieces, gravely brooding over her next move, unconscious of his presence as a man desiring her, and then to watch her bare arm stretched out over the board as she finally directed her knight on his crooked journey.

But Mariana was unwilling that he should always entertain her, and often asked him to have tea or dinner at her cottage. He liked to sit at the

other side of the hearth and watch her play with
the kitten on the floor. And looking up at tea on
some late, windy afternoon, liked to see the bare
boughs move across the glass in the wind, or at
night when they could no longer be seen, hear
them scratching on the pane like a restless ghost
outside.

And still, though they became more and more
aware of one another, no approach to greater
familiarity had taken place between them. But
Linschoten felt daily more attracted to Mariana,
and more conscious of her as a girl, and of himself as a man near her. He wondered if she would
let him make love to her, if it would make her
unhappy, if he would somehow injure her. Then
became uncertain of himself, remembered his wife
and felt disgust at the idea of being involved with
a woman. But making love to Mariana would not
be being involved with a woman; to him, he felt,
it would somehow be as clear and as impersonal
as bending down the bough of a flowering tree.

One night well on in the winter he had dinner
with her. She piled wood recklessly on the fire as
the hours went by, for the cold was biting outside,
but still he did not go. She put her last logs on the
fire and sat down on a cushion, leaning against
the chimney, for in the unceiled cottage the cold

seemed always to creep around and be at your back.

Linschoten had become very silent. The candles on the mantelpiece were burning low and still he did not go. The kitten had gone to sleep on the hearthrug and Mariana leaned over and stroked its ears to awake its little drowsy purr. Linschoten bent down and took her hand. She looked up at him questioningly, and he lifted her hand and kissed it and with his other hand smoothed back her hair. " Mariana," he said, " let me stay with you. Don't send me away—let me stay with you to-night." She looked at him silently, uncertain and unwilling, but not repelled.

He rose and drew her slowly to her feet until she was standing enclosed in his arms. He whispered again " Let me stay with you, Mariana; let me stay to-night."

She was unwilling and half frightened until looking at his face she was struck by an expression on it she had never seen there before. And when she allowed him to blow out the candles and lead her away, it was because of this that she went, because his face looked all at once so kind.

The bedroom door was latched outside to keep it from rattling in the wind, and this stopped them for a moment. And Mariana looked up again questioningly, uncertainly at his face clearly

visible in the firelight. And again she was struck
by the kindness of his look, and, reassured, put up
her hand to unlatch the door and let him lead
her in.

Late in the night, when Linschoten was asleep
beside her, Mariana lay troubled and unhappy.
She had been too shy to take pleasure in his short,
passionate embraces, they had both been so shy
with each other. Now she lay awake, her naked
body trembling a little with cold, though Linschoten's warm bare body lay almost touching.
Why did I let him embrace me ? she wondered
sadly. I did not want to. This is I who wanted one
lover, one love, lying by a strange man I do not
love. How did I come here ? I did not want this.

Quietly he slept, but she lay awake, very still
for fear of disturbing him, till the red, early sunlight began to stain the rough board walls like
wine. Then Linschoten awoke, and they smiled at
one another, embarrassed to find themselves
lying naked in one bed.

Mariana lay in bed long after he had gone. She
was profoundly melancholy. She thought it had
been sad enough to have one casual affair with
Holworth, but to have two within a few months
was shocking to her. It seemed to wound and to
spoil her very life-illusion. All day she sat tiredly

by the fire or wandered listlessly gathering dead branches in the wood, no longer diverted by even the kitten's charming pretence of great fear.

She knew that Linschoten would come in the afternoon and she did not want to see him. She felt shy and unwilling. And so when she heard his car on the road, she ran out of the cottage and hid in the woods behind a big tree trunk where some thick brambles grew. The kitten which loved to play hide-and-seek ran out too and hid behind a bush.

Linschoten waited but no one came, and called but no one answered, and he finally went away after writing a note and putting it with some flowers on the table. When he left the cottage, puzzled and disappointed by Mariana's absence, he did not know that four clear wild eyes watched him out of the wood.

But he caught Mariana in the field going to the spring for water the next afternoon and she asked him to stay for dinner. He felt baffled all the evening because she behaved precisely as if nothing had happened. Except that she was a little more reserved with him he could not see that his embraces had effected any change in her behaviour to him. She simply pretended that nothing had happened.

His own shyness made it difficult for him to

break through her reserve. He hardly knew how to proceed. He realised that they were in some ways too alike to be lovers. An affectionate, demonstrative, confident lover could break through Mariana's reserve, he felt, teach her to play like a vixen in a fern-bed, warm her and release her ; but he was more reserved even than she, and really needed some gay, not too delicate, experienced girl to put him at ease. But now it was the aloof Mariana that he wanted. Before the fire he took her in his arms and kissed her gently and sat holding her hand quietly in his. Presently he led her to the narrow couch under the big studio window. She did not refuse to go, but looked at him almost as if he puzzled her by his behaviour. He was daunted, but would not give up. He sat down beside her and began to kiss her and stroke her hair, and passed from kissing her lips to kissing the white, soft flesh at the neck of her dress, and then to stroking her knees and her round breasts under their slight silken covering. In a moment he was carried away and caught her in a closer embrace. She did not refuse him, but she did not respond to him. She was like a shy bride, he thought, who feels it her duty to let me do this incomprehensible thing to her. It was charming, and yet disappointing.

I wonder if I could ever teach her to love me and

to really respond to me, he thought again when it was over. And Mariana, rather like a little girl released from compulsion, sat by the fire, and they listened together to the wind in the woods and to the branch scratching like a cold ghost at the pane.

One evening, it was two months later and the bare trees were complaining in the winter wind, Mariana sat on the rug by John Linschoten's fire. They were alone in the house. Toru had gone to New York for a holiday, and Mariana was conscious of this isolation with Linschoten, closed with him in one house in the black darkness and the lonely fields, for she knew he meant her to spend the night with him. He had said with assumed carelessness as they got out of the car, "I'll just drain the radiator and put the car away for the night."

Since the time of their first embrace they had never spent a night together, and Mariana felt a strange excitement. To-night, she thought, we shall climb those stairs with the wind crying about us, and lie together naked in one bed. She shivered. Her body in the warmth of the fire was drowsy and half desirous. She had never in Linschoten's embraces felt any ecstasy ; but she was learning to take pleasure in his caresses. She

284

thought that the time might come when she would share his desire and its consummation. She was not sure. For some reason he always made her feel shy. He wanted her ; but he was reserved and sometimes almost cold. He seemed to restrain and beat down his desire, to try to make it take polite, formal shape. She wondered if they would ever be free together.

Linschoten began reading aloud to her :

> *I would I were an orange tree,*
> *That busy plant,*
> *So would I ever laden be,*
> *And never want*
> *Some fruit for him that planted me——*

He turned the pages—

> *Had we but world enough, and Time*
> *This coyness, lady, were no crime . . .*
> *The grave's a fine and private place*
> *But none, I think, do there embrace.*

She turned back to the sound of the poem flowing by and followed its stream to the last words :

> *But none, I think, do there embrace . . .*

Mariana's mind stayed while the poem went

on to its end. ' But none '—God, no !—the darkness—the cold—nothingness. Never mind, she said
to herself stoutly, you will not be there.

"What a beautiful thing that is," she said.
" Please go on reading. It is the hour for reading
aloud with the wind crying an accompaniment
outside, and the fire like a dog leaping up the
chimney at the cold." She was excited, happy.
She wanted to go on listening, to be moved again
by wonderful words. But Linschoten read :

> *At last the candle's out and now*
> *All that they had not done they do.*
> *What that is, who can tell ?*
> *But I believe it was no more*
> *Than thou and I have done before*
> *With Bridget and with Nell.*

He got up. " Shall we go to bed now, Mariana,"
he said. " It is late."

"Yes," she said. " I am sleepy." And he was
touched by her pretence that there was no special
meaning in his words, that they were to go to bed
only to sleep.

" I'll go up and see that your room is ready,"
he said. " Toru would be so grieved if anything
was lacking."

He went upstairs. Mariana slid from her chair
and sat on the fur rug, leaning her head against

286

the warm chimney corner and watching the flickering, wavering firelight.

The rhythm of the poetry had released her thoughts, and they flowed through her mind in a stream without her own volition.

I so wanted to love and be loved, she thought. I remember how I used to think I would be lonely in some other world if I did not find a lover in this. But I wanted to have only one lover and to love him always like the man in that Gaelic poem, ' The Red-Haired Man's Wife.'

I thought, my one love, there would be
But one house between you and me;
I thought I would find yourself nursing my child on
*   your knee—*
Over the waves I would leap with the leap of a swan
Till I came to the side of the wife of the red-haired
*   man—*

John Linschoten has red-hair—and a wife— her mind put in inconsequentially—and I am about to commit adultery. And she was suddenly amused at the idea of calling a staid night with Linschoten by so shocking a name.

For this—a voice of her mind continued, mocking her—people say you will go to Hell. I *will* go to Hell, she answered herself gaily—I will go to Hell like Auccassin with his pleasant companions, and I shall have lovers there, since I cannot find a true love anywhere, her mind added wistfully. Surely there will be some man without a girl who will have me ? Donne says : ' Loneliness is a torment we are not promised in Hell itself.' Surely I will not lack company in Hell ?

She heard Linschoten coming down the steps. " I must go to bed," she said to herself, reluctant to leave her peace by the warm fire. But the words made a picture in her mind of a garden bed in the spring which was coming, at the edge of a lawn embroidered with daisies like an English field. And it was as if she was already there, already passed through and beyond her relations with Linschoten.

She heard him at the door and rose slowly, absently, to her feet to go with him upstairs. But in her fancy she was still walking alone in the garden she had imagined and a morning wind was blowing : the sky was bright and brightening : there was a feeling of secret happiness in the air, of adventure about to begin.

THE END